Avenged to Death

A Jamie Brodie Mystery

The Jamie Brodie Mysteries

Cited to Death

Hoarded to Death

Burdened to Death

Researched to Death

Encountered to Death

There Goes the Neighborhood (bonus short story included with Encountered to Death)

Psyched to Death

Stacked to Death

Stoned to Death

High Desert and Low Country (bonus short stories included with Stoned to Death)

Talked to Death

Hearts and Best Men (bonus short stories included with Talked to Death)

Avenged to Death

Part 1

The best way to avenge thyself is not to become like the enemy. -
Marcus Aurelius

November 19, 1980

DEL MAR - A fatal crash on I-5 late last night took the lives of two women and seriously injured three others.

Tracy Jemison, 34, of Camp Pendleton, and Julie Brodie, 30, of Oceanside, were killed instantly when Jemison's Toyota Corolla was struck head on at high speed by a Ford Mustang traveling south in the northbound lane.

Two passengers in the back seat of the Corolla, Belinda Marcus, 33, and Marie Crabtree, 34, both of Camp Pendleton, were airlifted to UCSD Medical Center after being cut out of the vehicle. Both are in critical condition.

The driver of the Mustang was identified as Gavin Barkley, 20, of La Jolla.

He and his passenger, Kate Bianchi, 19, of Chula Vista, were also transported to UCSD Medical Center.

Barkley sustained a chest injury and is in fair condition. Bianchi was not wearing a seatbelt and was thrown through the windshield of the Mustang on impact.

She sustained severe head injuries and is in grave condition.

A California Highway Patrol officer at the scene said that the headlights on Barkley's car were not on.

The investigation is ongoing, but preliminary findings indicate that Barkley drove the wrong way up the off-ramp at the Del Mar Heights Rd. exit and struck Jemison's vehicle in the right lane.

Barkley's blood alcohol content at the time of the crash was 0.28%, nearly three times the legal limit.

The 5 northbound is still closed between the SR56 and Del Mar Heights Rd. exits and is expected to reopen by 10:00 am today.

"Dr. Brodie? I have a registered letter for you."

I looked up from my desk. Rick, our mailroom guy, was standing in my office doorway with an envelope.

"No kidding." This was a first. I signed Rick's clipboard and took the envelope from him. It was heavy stock, thick with pages, creamy white in color. "What the heck is it?"

"Dunno." Rick took his clipboard back. "Have a good day."

I leaned against the door frame as I studied the envelope.

Jeremy D. Brodie, D.Phil.

Charles E. Young Research Library

University of California, Los Angeles

Los Angeles, CA 90095

I recognized the return address as downtown San Diego. The sender sounded like a law firm: Smith, Hendrickson, Delio and Franklin, LLC.

I went next door to Liz Nguyen's office and waved the envelope at her. "I got a registered letter."

"Who from?"

"It looks like a law firm."

"It looks like? Open it, ya goof." She handed me her letter opener.

I slit the envelope and removed the pages inside. "It's a will."

LAST WILL AND TESTAMENT
OF
RANDALL CHESTERSON BARKLEY

I, Randall Chesterson Barkley, now residing in the County of San Diego, State of California, and being of sound mind and memory and not acting under fraud, menace, duress or the undue influence of any person whomsoever, do hereby make, publish and declare this to be my Last Will and

**Testament, and hereby expressly revoke any and all former wills
and codicils to wills heretofore made by me…**

A lot of legalese followed. I flipped through the pages. "Who
the hell is Randall Chesterson Barkley?"

Liz stood and looked over my shoulder. "You don't know?"

"Never heard of him."

"The lawyers are in San Diego - is it someone you knew as a
kid?"

"Not that I remember. And even if it was, why have they sent
me his will?"

Liz went back to her computer and opened UCLA's database
page. "Maybe his obituary was in the San Diego paper."

"Maybe." I went to look over her shoulder.

It didn't take her long to find it.

*Randall Chesterson Barkley, 85, passed away February 16,
2014, after a long illness. Mr. Barkley was a native of San Diego, a
graduate of Stanford University, and the founder of Zaltu Inc. He
was predeceased by his wife of forty-two years, Jeanette Cordelia
Graham Barkley. There are no other survivors. In lieu of flowers,
please donate to Hospice.*

I said, "He died over a year ago."

Liz said, "His name doesn't ring any bells? He wasn't your
Little League coach or anything?"

"Nope."

"Maybe your dad knows." Liz gathered some papers. "I've
got to lead a research session. Let me know."

"I will." I went back to my office to get my phone and found
a text from my brother Kevin. *You free? Call me.*

I called. "What's up?"

"I got something odd in the mail today, delivered to the
station."

"A copy of the will of Randall Chesterson Barkley, whoever the hell that is?"

"Yeah. You don't recognize that name?"

"No. Do you?"

"Nope."

"Liz suggested that Dad might know."

"Good idea. Do you have time to call him? Jon and I are about to head out to a scene."

"Yeah, I'll call."

"Text me."

"I will."

I closed my office door and called my dad. When he answered, it sounded like he was outside. "Hey, Dad. Whatcha doin'?"

"I'm at the beach with Colin. We're taking pictures of plants."

"Ah." My nephew Colin was being homeschooled through middle school by his parents, my brother Jeff and sister-in-law Valerie. My dad, retired from the Marine Corps, helped out frequently with the field work. "I just have a quick question."

"What's up?"

I explained. "Does the name Randall Chesterson Barkley mean anything to you?"

Dead silence. I began to think my phone had dropped the call. "Dad?"

He said softly, "Randall Barkley was the father of the man who killed your mom."

I sucked in my breath. "*What??*"

Another moment of silence. I could hear Colin's voice in the background, telling my dad something. Dad said, "I'll call you tonight. You going to be home?"

"Yeah."

"Okay. Talk to you then."

Holy fucking shit. The man whose son had caused the fatal car crash that killed my mom - and Kevin and I had a copy of his will? I flipped through the pages again, and something caught my eye.

My own name.

I hereby give, or devise and bequeath all of my property and estate, both real and personal, and wheresoever or howsoever situated, or to which I may be entitled at the time of my death, to be divided into equal shares, among the following:

Jeffrey David Brodie
Kevin Cole Brodie
Jeremy Douglas Brodie
Alexandra Colleen Crabtree
Asher Finn Crabtree
Drew Harris Jemison
Jennifer Louisa Jemison McCune
Joshua William Marcus
Karen Elizabeth Marcus Fornari
Jennelle Renae Shifflett

Who were these other people? I knew my mom had been with some of her friends the night she was killed. I looked at the other names - Crabtree, Jemison, Marcus, Shifflett - but didn't recognize them.

Were they the children of my mom's friends?

I flipped through the rest of the will, but there was no mention of anyone else. Randall Barkley's wife had died before him; there were no other survivors, according to the obituary.

What happened to his son?

I had never heard of Zaltu, Inc. I looked it up online - and nearly fell out of my chair.

Randall Barkley had founded Zaltu, Inc., a software company that wrote code for military satellites, in 1973. The company had done well during the Cold War, stagnated in the 1990s, then took off again after 9/11. In 2003 Barkley sold the company to Lockheed Martin for $600 million.

I blinked and shook my head to make sure I was seeing that figure right.

Six hundred million dollars.

There were ten names on the list of heirs.

Sixty million dollars apiece.

Suddenly I couldn't breathe. I grabbed my inhaler and took a puff.

Then I called my friend - my attorney - Melanie Hayes.

Mel was in court; I left a message with Sunny, the firm's legal secretary. I texted Kevin - *It's complicated, call me* - then called my fiancé, Pete. His phone went straight to voicemail. *Shit.* I wanted someone to talk to *now*. I glanced at the clock; he should be doing office hours. I took a chance and dialed his office number.

He sounded warm but professional. "Psychology department, Dr. Ferguson."

"Hey."

His voice brightened considerably. "Hey, yourself. What's up?"

"I tried your cell, but it's off."

"Yeah, I've got office hours, but there's no one here. You okay? You sound short of breath."

"I am short of breath. I think I may have just inherited sixty million dollars."

He laughed. "Good one. What are you all smoking over there?"

"I'm serious." I told him about the will. "Six hundred million, divided ten ways. I don't - I can't - it's not -"

"Good God. Did you call Mel?"

"Had to leave a message."

"Okay. Let's not get excited until she finds out what this is all about."

"It looks like a legal will."

"Yeah, but he may have spent his fortune down to nothing. Don't start buying up waterfront property just yet."

"I won't."

When I met Liz at the research desk for our 1:00 shift, she said, "Did your dad know what that will was about?"

I lowered my voice and told her. When I got to the $600 million part, she breathed, "Holy *shit*."

"But that was years ago. He may have spent it all."

Liz disagreed. "Nah. A guy like that who built a business from the ground up? He hasn't spent it all. He worked too hard to make it."

"Why would he leave it to us, though?"

She shrugged, as if the answer was obvious. "Guilt."

I said, "Don't tell anyone. If it is a lot of money, I don't want people here to know. At least not yet."

"I won't." She was nearly whispering now. "Will you quit your job?"

"It's *way* too early to be thinking in those terms."

Someone cleared his throat; I looked up to see Clinton Kenneally standing before us. Liz said, "Oh, sorry. Hi, Clinton."

He bestowed a gentle smile on us. "Good afternoon, Ms. Nguyen, Dr. Brodie. The word of the day is *manumit*." He bowed and walked away.

I opened an online dictionary and found the definition. "To free from slavery."

Liz said, "With sixty million dollars, you'd be pretty damn free."

I had just stepped onto the bus, on my way home, when Mel called back. "Hey, Jamie. What's up?"

I told her about the will. "This can't be real, can it?"

"I'll find out. Let me call the law firm right now."

She called me back as I was walking from the bus stop to the townhouse that I owned with Pete. "I spoke to the senior partner's paralegal. The will is legitimate and has cleared probate, so the assets will be distributed soon."

"Who are the other people?"

"The paralegal didn't have any other information. Apparently old man Barkley only did business with Gordon Smith himself." I heard voices in the background over the phone. "My next client's here. I'll talk to you later."

After dinner, I was placing the last dish in the drainer when my dad called. "Hey, sport. Sorry I couldn't talk earlier."

"Oh, it's fine. I called Mel." I recounted my conversation with her. "I wondered if the other names on the list might be the children of Mom's friends."

"What were the names?"

"The last names were Crabtree, Jemison, Marcus, and Shifflett."

"Marie Crabtree, Tracy Jemison and Belinda Marcus were your mom's friends. I don't recognize the name Shifflett."

"Were they all killed?"

"No. Tracy was. She was driving, and your mom was in the front seat. Belinda was paralyzed from the neck down. Marie broke both legs and nearly bled to death, but she recovered eventually."

"Have you kept in touch with them?"

My dad's voice was heavy. "No. I tried, but…" He trailed off.

I said softly, "It was too hard."

"Yeah."

"Liz and I looked up the old man's obituary. It said he had no survivors. What happened to his son?"

"As far as I know he's still in jail, but I haven't kept track. I suppose he could have died in prison."

"How old would he be now?"

Dad paused to do a quick calculation. "Fifty-five."

"Why would Barkley leave his money to us?"

"I have no idea. He spent enough of it defending his son at trial - I don't know why he'd leave it to you all now."

"Dad… What happened?"

He sighed. "Barkley - Gavin Barkley, the son - was driving so drunk he could barely stand, according to the friends at the party he'd just left. He drove the wrong way up the off ramp at the Del Mar Road exit with his lights off and hit Tracy's car head on at full speed. She never had a chance to put on the brakes."

I took in a deep breath and blew it out. "Was Gavin even injured?"

"He bruised his heart and broke some ribs, but he recovered pretty quickly. His girlfriend didn't have her seatbelt on and went through his windshield. She had a severe head injury and ended up in a permanent vegetative state."

"How did it even go to trial?"

"The kid pled not guilty. Old man Barkley paid for the best defense attorneys. He had a whole team. It looked for a while like the kid might get off."

"What happened?"

"The prosecutor started bringing us in. Marie was still in a wheelchair at the time, and she testified first. Then Tracy's husband, Tony, brought his kids in. They were a few years older than you all, and the prosecutor put Drew - the oldest - on the stand. Then he asked me to bring you guys to court."

"Why? We were so little."

"That's why. So the jury could see what Barkley had done. I dressed you three so you matched, in little khaki shorts and blue polo shirts. Dad came with me. I carried you and held Jeff's hand, and

Dad carried Kevin. When they saw you, everyone in the courtroom went 'ohhhh' at the same time."

"Did you testify?"

"Only at the sentencing phase."

"Did the paralyzed lady testify?"

"Belinda. She sure did. She was still in a halo, but she could speak just fine. Then the girlfriend's parents brought her in, and that was the last straw for the jury. They were nearly all crying." Another sigh. "It was brutal, what the prosecutor did, but it worked. The jury recommended the maximum sentence on all counts, and that's what the judge gave him."

"Good."

My dad barked a laugh. "Yeah. It was."

"Are the other families still in town?"

"I don't know. Do you want me to find out?"

"No, no." I'd find out some other way. I didn't want to put my dad through anything more. "I'm sorry to ask you all these questions."

"It's okay. You have a right to know what happened."

"I've always been afraid to ask."

I could hear the smile in my dad's voice. "I know, sport."

I spent the rest of the evening on the phone - first with Jeff and Kevin, repeating all the information I'd gathered. Jeff was dismissive of the will. "There's no way the old guy would leave us all that money. I bet he left the bulk of it to some charity and we each get a token amount."

"I don't know… I didn't see any charities listed."

Jeff made a "pah" sound. "We'll see. I guarantee, he tossed some pittance our way to assuage his guilty conscience."

"Maybe. But hell, someone dumps a couple of thousand bucks in my lap, I'm not turning it down."

He just snorted.

When I called Kevin, he said, "Gavin Barkley, huh? I can find out if he's still in jail."

"Will you? I'd like to know."

"Sure. I'd like to know too."

"Jeff thinks there must be a catch. We won't get that much."

"Nah. I know how to read legal documents now, remember?" Kevin had just completed a year of paralegal training and earned his certificate; he worked for Mel on the side. "I read every word of that will this afternoon. There are no other beneficiaries. The only question is, how big is the estate?"

I said, "I sure would like to find that out."

"So would I."

My last conversation of the evening was with my friend Ali's dad, Charlie Fortner. Charlie and my dad had worked together at Pendleton for years, until Dad retired in 2002. Charlie had finally retired a few years ago. He and Ali's mom still lived in the same house where Ali and her sister Lauren had grown up, only a half mile from my dad's place.

I'd spent almost as much time at the Fortners' growing up as I had at my own house. Ali's parents had held out hope that Ali and I might end up together, until Ali and I both came out to them in high school. After their initial shock, they'd accepted the news, and I'd stayed close to Ali's parents.

I wasn't sure the Fortners would be home. They spent about half the year in their RV traveling all over the US and Canada. But I got lucky.

Charlie answered the phone. I said, "Hey, Mr. Fortner, it's Jamie."

"Jamie! How are you?"

"Fine, sir, thanks. I'm surprised to find you home. I thought you might be someplace more interesting."

He laughed. "Nah, had to come home and refuel. What's up?"

"How hard would it be for you to find out if three men who served at Pendleton are still in town?"

"Not hard at all. I've got a friend in personnel at the base. But your dad could find out as easily as I could."

"I know, but I don't want to ask him. And I don't actually know the names of the Marines themselves, just their wives."

"Okay, you've got my curiosity up. What are the names?"

"Belinda Marcus, Marie Crabtree and Tracy Jemison."

Charlie was quiet for a moment. "Ah. I see why you don't want to ask your dad."

"He's the one who gave me their names, but I figured that was enough."

"Sure." It sounded like Charlie was looking for a pen. "I didn't know any of the husbands myself, but my buddy in personnel has been there forever. He'll know."

"Thanks, Mr. Fortner. I appreciate it."

"No problem, son. I'll let you know what I find out."

I tossed the phone onto the sofa and blew out a breath. Pete glanced up at me from his laptop. "Find out anything?"

"Just that Kevin read the entire will and there are no other beneficiaries."

"Jeff doesn't think it's real?"

"He's skeptical. I have to admit, so am I."

"Why?"

I considered. "It just doesn't seem possible. It's too unreal."

"It's certainly out of the bounds of normal."

"You can say that again."

He grinned. "It's certainly out of the bounds of normal."

"Ha ha." I pulled off one of my socks and threw it at him; it came to rest, draped nicely over his computer screen. "What are you doing?"

"Grading." He picked my sock off his computer and tossed it to the floor.

I looked around the room. We were in our office, which also served in a pinch as a guest bedroom. Pete was at the long, narrow table that served as our desk, at "his" end, the lamp casting a warm glow on his dark brown hair. Behind him, the mahogany finish on a wall of built-in bookshelves and cabinets reflected the light. I was sprawled on the cushy leather sofa which opened into an incredibly comfortable bed.

We'd completely remodeled this room about a year ago and had been delighted with the results. I said, "I love this room."

"Mm. Me too."

"If this inheritance ends up being just a few thousand dollars, even, we should remodel our bathroom."

He glanced up at me again. "If that's how you want to use the money."

"Hey, it's a joint decision, right?"

He gave me a look. "That's not what you said when I was trying to convince you that you could share my salary."

Pete made significantly more money than I did. I'd been teaching classes as an adjunct in the history department to make up the difference. "Salary is different. This is a one-time thing. What would I use it on for myself?"

"You could get a car." We'd been living with one vehicle, Pete's 1998 Jeep Cherokee.

"I don't want a car. I want a walk-in shower."

He turned back to his laptop, an indulgent smile on his face. "You probably shouldn't speculate until you find out how much money's involved."

"I know." I took off my other sock and threw it at him; this time it landed right on his keyboard. "Are you about done?"

"Good God. I'm gonna have to sterilize this laptop." He tossed my second sock after the first.

"I thought you liked my feet."

He leered at me over the rim of the screen. "I like other parts better."

"Uh huh. Like I said, are you about done? Or do I have to throw my tighty whities over there?"

He grinned and closed the laptop.

Tuesday, March 31

That night, I dreamed that the Prize Patrol from Publishers Clearinghouse showed up at our front door to deliver my inheritance: a crisp twenty-dollar bill.

I was walking from the bus stop to the library when Kevin called. "Gavin Barkley is still in Folsom. He's served thirty-four years of a forty year sentence."

"He'll get out in a few years."

"He's getting out in two weeks. He's been granted parole."

"*Oh*. Listen, we've got to find out what's going on with this will. If Mel can get us in to see the attorney, do you want to go?"

"Absolutely. I'll take a personal day."

"Did you call Jeff about Gavin Barkley?"

"No. Can you do that? Jon and I have an autopsy this morning."

"Sure."

I had to leave a message with Jeff's receptionist, but he called me back in about a half hour. "Kevin found the guy?"

"Yeah, he's in Folsom Prison. He's getting paroled in two weeks."

Jeff snorted with disgust. "He should have been put away for life."

"Yeah, he should. Listen, I'm going to ask Mel to get an appointment for us with the attorney, to get our questions answered. You interested?"

He hesitated for a minute, then said, "Sure. Let me know when you've got it set up."

I didn't get a chance to speak to Liz until we were at the reference desk. We were moderately busy, but I managed to fill her in on what I'd learned about the Barkleys. When I told her about the accident, her eyes widened. "Holy cow. They didn't go after the host of the party?"

"This was 1980. I don't think that was done yet. They should have, though. Barkley was under age."

"When did the drinking age become twenty-one in California?"

"It's always been twenty-one here."

Clinton approached, and we turned toward him. Liz said, "Hi, Clinton."

He smiled. "The word of the day is *aleatory*." He bowed and walked away.

I found the definition. "Characterized by chance or random elements."

Liz rested her chin on her fist. "Like your mom's accident. If they'd left the movies fifteen minutes later, it wouldn't have been their car that Barkley hit."

I said, "There is no such thing as accident; it is fate misnamed."

Liz gave me a sharp look. "Shakespeare?"

"Napoleon."

She grinned and turned to the student approaching the desk. "Hi, can I help you?"

During this spring quarter, I was teaching a graduate class, Topics in Ancient History, Tuesday and Thursday afternoons from 3:00 to 4:15. My routine was to work until 6:15 to make up the time difference, since the teaching gig wasn't part of my job description. Usually I had rugby practice on Tuesday and Thursday evenings, but I'd dislocated my left shoulder in a game three weeks ago. It was healing as expected, but the injury had ended my season. I'd just gotten out of the sling on Friday.

When I got home, it was nearly seven, and I was ravenous. I dropped my computer bag on the landing and greeted Pete, who was setting our small kitchen table. "What's for dinner?"

"Leek and potato soup." Pete filled two bowls and carried them to the table.

I inhaled deeply. "Man, that smells good. Thank you."

"You're welcome. Anything new?"

"Mm." I slurped my first spoonful of soup. "Kevin found Gavin Barkley. He's in Folsom."

Pete started singing. "I hear the train a'comin'; it's rolling round the bend…"

"Yeah, well, Gavin isn't going to be stuck in Folsom Prison much longer. He's being paroled in two weeks."

He sobered immediately. "The timing of that is quite the coincidence."

"You think there's something to it?"

"Probably not. His parole hearing had to have been at least four months ago. How could he have known when the estate would be distributed?"

"I suppose the attorney could have told him."

Pete scratched his chin. "Maybe he intends to contest the will. That would be a lot easier to do from the outside."

"Hoo boy. If by some chance the estate is a big one - that could piss people off."

He shot me a glance. "Would you be pissed?"

I thought about that. "Nah. My life's awesome enough. I wouldn't miss money I'd never had."

Pete chuckled. "Glad to hear that."

Wednesday, April 1

The next morning, I called Mel as soon as I got off the bus, hoping to catch her before she began seeing clients, and got lucky. When she answered she said, "Hey, rich boy."

I laughed. "No way. Actually, that's why I'm calling. Jeff, Kevin and I want to make an appointment with the attorney to find out exactly what we're dealing with. Is that possible?"

"Sure. Do you want me to set it up?"

"If you can, that'd be great. For next week sometime. Preferably in the morning, although I know his schedule might be tight."

"I'll see what I can do."

She called back in a couple of hours. "You have a meeting arranged with Gordon Smith at his office on Monday at noon. It's his lunch hour, but he's squeezing you in."

"Wow. How'd you pull that off?"

"As it turns out, Smith's legal assistant is Michelle Richardson, from high school."

Michelle Richardson had graduated with us and had been in a lot of our AP classes. "No kidding! So she did us a favor."

"Yup. She's going to call the other local beneficiaries and tell them there's a Q and A session at that time. You may have a couple of other people show up."

"That's fine. Thanks, Mel, you're the best."

"Yes, I am. Tell Michelle thank you when you see her."

"I certainly will."

I called Kevin and Jeff immediately so they could make plans to take the time off. I left the message at Jeff's office with his receptionist, who said she'd take care of it. When I called Kevin's number, it was his partner, Jon Eckhoff, who answered. "Doctor Brodie. Why aren't you working?"

"Detective Eckhoff. Why aren't you driving?" Kevin usually had Jon drive when they were out and about; Jon had hyperactive tendencies, particularly when forced to sit still. Kevin tried to ward off the finger-tapping, knee-jiggling and pens-as-drumsticks-on-the-dashboard by making Jon take the wheel.

"Himself had a bad night at home. He wanted to drive so he'd have something else on which to concentrate."

"Crap." Kevin and his longtime girlfriend, Abby Glenn, had been having problems, escalating in severity for several months. "Please tell him that we have an appointment with the lawyer in San Diego next Monday, if he can take a personal day."

"Okie dokie. I'll make sure he does it."

"Thanks, Jon."

"You're welcome. Tell my lovely Liz hello."

"Will do."

That evening I had my own grading to do. Pete and I sat next to each other at our elongated desk, working in harmonious silence. I finished before Pete - my class wasn't large, and I was only grading discussion posts - and started thinking about money.

If I really was going to get sixty million dollars, what would I do?

My initial reaction was to hang onto it. Pete and I were edging toward middle age - what if one of us got sick or was injured as badly as my mom's friends had been? Medical bills could easily lead to bankruptcy.

But a couple of million ought to cover that contingency. What else?

I truly didn't want a car. I rode the bus to work; Pete walked to work. Anyplace else we went was usually together. We didn't need two cars.

I could use a new pair of rugby cleats…

My mind was wandering when the desk began to vibrate.

Earthquake. A small one, fortunately. Pete didn't even look up. When the shaking stopped, he said, "Three point eight."

I laughed. Guessing the magnitude of earthquakes was a game for Pete, who'd grown up in Lancaster, practically on top of the San Andreas Fault. He excelled at it; I wouldn't bet against him.

But it gave me an idea. If The Big One hit, and LA was torn to pieces, we'd need a place to go. Someplace far from the Ring of Fire around the Pacific Rim.

A second home. A refuge. A place with two requirements: out of the earthquake zone but in a state with marriage equality.

Pete's brother Steve lived in such a place. Alamogordo, New Mexico.

I opened a new browser tab and started looking at property.

Thursday, April 2

That night, I dreamed that an earthquake struck while I was at work. Damage was extensive, although miraculously the buses were still running. I got home to find Pete searching through the rubble. I said, "What are you looking for?"

"Our tent."

"We don't have a tent."

"Oh." He straightened up. "Then we'd better start walking."

I woke up thinking, *We need a tent.*

Charlie Fortner called me as I was heading for the reference desk. "I found the Marines you asked about. Brian and Belinda Marcus are still in town, in an assisted living villa. Rick Crabtree is retired, and he and Marie live in Atlanta. Tony Jemison remarried and then divorced the second wife. He retired to a small farm up in western Oregon." He paused, then said, "I checked. Brian Marcus is in the phone book."

"Thanks, Mr. Fortner. I appreciate it." I dropped into my seat at the desk and sighed.

Liz said, "What's up?"

"I have a decision to make." I told her about the Marcuses. "I want to talk to someone who knew my mom. But I don't want to upset them or my dad."

"I'd think your dad would understand. And what's the worst that could happen? You call these folks and they hang up on you?"

"I guess I'll run it by Pete. See what he thinks."

We had a short burst of activity at the desk, and Clinton had to wait a couple of minutes when he arrived. When he was finally able to approach the desk, he smiled. "The word of the day is *nostomania.*"

Liz looked it up. "An irresistible compulsion to return home." She poked me in the elbow. "That's Clinton telling you it's okay to call your mom's friend."

I poked her back. "To quote Clinton himself, 'Sometimes a word is just a word.'"

Liz, as usual, got the *last* word. "Not this time."

As we washed dishes that evening, I asked Pete, "Is it inappropriate that I want to meet my mom's friend?"

"Not at all. She's someone else who knew your mom. It's natural that you'd want to seek her out."

"Do you think my dad will mind?"

"I think he'll understand."

"Do you think Mrs. Marcus will be upset?"

He gave me a look. "You won't know until you call, will you?"

"Okay, okay." I dried my hands and dialed the number.

A man's voice answered. "Hello?"

"Hello. Is this Mr. Marcus?"

"Yes, who's calling?"

"My name is Jamie Brodie. I'm Dave and Julie Brodie's youngest son."

His tone changed immediately from suspicion to recognition. "Yes, Jamie! My God, Belinda and I were just talking about you and your brothers earlier today, wondering what had become of you. How are you?"

Relief washed through me. "Fine, sir, thank you. I suppose your children received copies of Randall Barkley's will."

"They did." He hesitated for a second. "Anyway. What can I do for you?"

"I just recently learned your names and - I wanted to meet someone else who knew my mom."

"Of course, son, we'd love to have you visit. Are you in town?"

"No, sir. I'm in Los Angeles. It would have to be Saturday or Sunday."

"Saturday's fine. Not too early, though."

"Oh, no, sir, I have to drive down that morning. Is eleven okay?"

"That's perfect." His tone expressed nothing but delight. "Belinda will be thrilled."

"I'm looking forward to it, too. I'll see you then." I hung up and looked at Pete. "Saturday at eleven."

"Good." Pete nodded at my phone. "You'd better tell your dad."

I was hesitant to tell Dad what I'd done, but I steeled myself with Pete's assurance that he'd understand and dialed the number. He answered almost immediately. "Hey, sport."

"Hey, Dad. Am I interrupting anything?"

"Not at all. Barb and I are just relaxing on the porch."

"Tell Barb hi."

He did. "She says hi back. What's up?"

I took a deep breath. "Well, I've done something, and I don't know how you'll feel about it. So I wanted to tell you."

"Okay…?"

"I asked Charlie Fortner to find out if any of the other families from the accident were still around. The Marcuses are right there in Oceanside, and they have a listed number. I called and talked to Mr. Marcus - and I'm going to see them Saturday."

My dad was quiet for a moment, but not long. "That's fine, sport. You could have asked me to find out for you."

"I know, but I didn't want to put you through that."

He sighed. "Jamie, it's okay. You don't have to handle me so carefully."

"What if I want to handle you carefully?"

He chuckled. "Well, that's okay, too. I suppose it's natural for you to want to talk to someone else who knew your mom."

"That's what Pete said."

"If the psychologist says so, it must be true. How did Brian sound?"

"He sounded fine. Did you know him well?"

"Yes. Charlie and I were both in his chain of command."

"Was he an officer?"

"Yep. At the time he was a major."

"What about Mrs. Marcus?"

"Belinda was a sweetheart. Tracy Jemison was your mom's best friend, but Belinda was a close second. Will you stop by here afterwards?"

"Yes, sir."

When I hung up, Pete said, "You're going to Oceanside on Saturday and San Diego on Monday? That's a lot of back and forth."

"Ah, you're right. Do you want to spend the weekend down there?"

"If your dad doesn't mind."

I called Dad back and explained the situation. "How would you feel about having houseguests for the weekend?"

He laughed. "I'll put you to work."

"I'd expect no less. We'll see you Saturday morning."

Friday, April 3

The week had begun with one shock in the mail. It ended with another.

It was customary for Liz and me to check our mailboxes after our reference shift. I had the usual mix of university press catalogs and flyers for new encyclopedia sets - and a letter.

Return address, Folsom Prison.

I stood for a second, staring at the envelope. Liz noticed my frozen state and said, "What is it?"

I showed it to her. "Let's go upstairs to open this."

We went into my office and closed the door. Liz said, "Is it from *him?*"

"Who else could it be?" I tore open the envelope and extracted the one-page, handwritten letter.

Dear Dr. Brodie,

My name is Gavin Barkley, and I am the man responsible for your mother's death. I understand from Gordon Smith that you have received your copy of my father's will. I wish to assure you that I do not intend to challenge the will. I have no desire to profit from any of my father's dealings.

I am being released on parole in two weeks. At that time, I intend to make a fresh start of my life. As part of that process, I would like the opportunity to meet you in person, to apologize for my past transgressions.

If you wish to have nothing to do with me, I understand. I simply ask your forgiveness. However, I hope that you will allow me to do this in a more meaningful fashion - face to face.

I have added your name - and the names of the other heirs - to my list of approved visitors. I have included instructions for making an appointment to visit the prison.

Thank you for your consideration.

Gavin Barkley

Liz's eyes were wide. "Holy *crap*. Does he really think any of you are going to make that trip?"

"I don't know." I stared at the letter in my hand. "This is bizarre."

"Why dredge up the past like this?"

"His past is ending." I shrugged. "I understand if he wants to move into the future with a lighter load on his conscience."

Liz looked skeptical. "Do you want to allow him to do that?"

I didn't have an answer.

Pete and I had begun a tradition last fall of keeping Friday evenings as Date Nights. We usually went out to dinner, just the two of us, as a reward for making it to the end of the week. So when Kevin called as I was walking in our front door Friday after work, I was hoping he didn't want to talk long.

My hope was unrealized.

Kevin asked, "Did you get Barkley's letter today?"

"Yeah. I don't even know what to think about it."

He snorted. "There's nothing *to* think. Mine went right into File Thirteen. What are you guys doing this evening?"

I closed the front door behind me. Pete was lounging on the sofa, watching the news. I said, "Um - it's date night."

Pete gave me a questioning look; I mouthed "Kevin" to him. He sat up, frowning.

Kevin said, "Oh." He sounded disappointed.

I said, "Why? What's up?"

"Nothing… Abby supposedly has to work late, and I'm not in the mood to go home. But I know, it's Friday night. I shouldn't have called."

I raised my eyebrows at Pete, questioning. He rolled his eyes, then smiled and waved his hand in a "come on" motion. I said,

"Why don't you meet us at the Indian place around the corner from the house?"

"Do they have beer?"

"Indian beer, sure."

"Good enough. I'll see you there."

I hung up. Pete said, "Where's Abby?"

"Working late. Or so she says."

"On a Friday?"

"Who knows what she's actually doing?" Abby was a carpenter, whose crew built sets for TV and movie studios. She'd been claiming for months that she had to work overtime. Frequently. In the first six years of their relationship, she'd hardly ever worked overtime. When Kevin asked her about the set being built that was requiring all the overtime, she was evasive.

We all thought something else was going on, but it didn't seem that Kevin had the heart to investigate.

Pete and I were seated at the restaurant, working on our first beer, when Kevin came in. He dropped tiredly into the chair opposite us. "I'm sorry about barging in on your date night, guys. I won't do it again."

Pete waved that off. "No worries. We'll have two Date Nights next week."

Kevin smiled weakly. I said, "Is Abby working on an overdue production?"

"She claims to be."

"But she won't tell you the details."

"No." Kevin sighed and looked out the window. "She always used to tell me about everything they built. We used to go to the movies to see her work. Now..." He trailed off.

Pete said, "Are you not talking much?"

"Oh, we're talking." The server brought Kevin's beer; he took a drink then began to pick at the label. "If arguing counts as talking."

I saw Pete subtly shift from friend to psychologist. "What are you arguing about?"

"Everything." More label picking. "It used to be just my schedule. Now it seems like I can't do anything right."

I said, "She should be happy now that you're done with school." Kevin's paralegal classes had met every Tuesday and Thursday evening for eleven months. Abby had complained incessantly about Kevin's absence, even though he was doing it so they could afford the mortgage on the house with the workshop that Abby had wanted.

"She's not."

Pete said, "But when she has to work late, it's a different story, isn't it?"

Kevin barked a laugh. "Of course." He shook his head. "She's not working overtime."

I said, "Do you think she's going to Andie's?"

"Yep."

Abby was the third of five daughters. Andie - Andrea - was the oldest. She was a bitchy control freak who had always disliked Kevin. I said, "Nothing good can come of that."

Pete asked, "How long has this been going on? Since you started classes?"

Kevin shook his head, gently pushing the shredded bits of label into a tiny mound. "Since I shot Hunter Mitchell."

Pete and I looked at each other in alarm. I said, "I thought…"

"You thought she'd been supportive through that." Kevin smiled, but it was more of a grimace. "That night, after you called her? It took her three hours to get home. She arrived after Dad did. Dad and I talked, but she didn't say a word all night. She barely mentioned it the next day. At the time, I just thought it had taken her that long to finish at work."

I said, "She told me she was leaving for home as soon as I called her."

"A couple of weeks ago I asked her where she'd gone that night. She'd been freaked out and didn't want me to know, so she'd gone to Andie's first, to get her advice on how to handle the situation."

Pete said, "God knows what Andie said about that."

Kevin took a long drink of beer. "She said I was a murderer."

I groaned. Pete said, "Kev. You are not a murderer."

"I get that. But, you know, something like that happens, you expect support from your partner, not accusation." He sighed deeply. "I still love her. I'm pretty sure she doesn't feel the same about me."

My heart was breaking for Kevin. I couldn't begin to know what to say. Pete started to speak but hesitated when our server approached.

Kevin had taken off his jacket and hung it over the back of his chair. He wore his service weapon at his waist rather than in a shoulder holster, so it wasn't obvious that he was armed - but our server noticed it anyway. He said, "Oh, police! There is no charge for you."

Kevin looked up in surprise. "Oh, no. I'm not Santa Monica police, I'm LAPD."

"It does not matter. Police officers eat free. Anything you like."

Kevin smiled. "Thank you."

The server had given us a chance to change the subject. I said, "Do you get that much?"

"Not as much as we used to." Kevin grinned reminiscently. "Pete, remember the coffee shop in Brentwood?"

Pete laughed. "I certainly do."

Pete had been Kevin's first partner on the force, the only partner he'd had as a patrol officer. They'd worked together five years. I thought I'd heard all their stories, but they started telling new ones. Pretty soon we were all laughing, including Kevin.

I figured it was worth giving up date night to get Kevin to laugh.

Saturday, April 4

That night, I dreamed that Abby and her sisters were running a drug smuggling ring. Pete and I discovered it because they were distributing product to their dealers in our back alley. We called 911, which should have brought the Santa Monica cops, but Kevin showed up. All five women jumped him. Abby was yelling, "You can't arrest us! This is Santa Monica! You're LAPD!"

Before Pete and I could make it down the stairs to help him, I woke up.

We went for a run and ate breakfast, then packed quickly and drove to Oceanside. I dropped Pete at my dad's house and then went to meet Belinda Marcus.

El Camino Assisted Living was a one-story Spanish-style building on a bluff overlooking downtown Oceanside and the pier. The central building had two wings, and there were a series of small duplex cottages on either side of the center. It was light, bright and beautifully landscaped.

If you had to be in assisted living, this wouldn't be a bad place for it.

Belinda Marcus lived in the first cottage left of the central building. There was a van with a handicap plate parked in the broad driveway and a sidewalk gently sloping to the front door. I rang the doorbell, and the door was opened by a handsome older man in a polo shirt and jeans. I said, "Mr. Marcus? I'm Jamie Brodie."

He beamed. "Yes, of course. I'm so glad to see you. Please come in." He showed me into the foyer, a wide, tile-covered space running to the back of the house, where French doors were open. I could see flowers beyond. "Belinda's out back. Can I get you something to drink? Iced tea?"

"Yes, sir, thank you."

The kitchen was to the left of the central passage. Mr. Marcus turned into it. "I'll get your tea. You go on outside."

I stepped out the back door into a floral paradise. It reminded me of the British gardens I'd seen when living in England. A woman in a wheelchair - Belinda - was sitting beside a small table, speaking to a dark-haired young woman in a pink scrub suit. Belinda rolled forward a bit. "Jamie?"

"Yes, ma'am."

Pink Scrubs smiled at me and went into the house. Belinda lifted her left arm at the shoulder, reaching toward me. Her hand wasn't entirely limp, but she didn't have much grip. I took her hand and squeezed it gently.

Belinda was an attractive woman, her salt-and-pepper hair pulled back into a ponytail. "Goodness, look at you. I haven't seen you since you were barely two years old, but I'd know you anywhere. Sit down, sit down." She placed her left hand on the controls of her chair and turned it so that it faced one of the seats on the patio. "I'm so happy that you called."

I said, "I should have come before, but I didn't know your name. I only learned the details of the accident recently."

Mr. Marcus appeared with a tray holding three glasses of tea, one with a straw. He held it for Belinda, who took a drink. "Mm. Thanks, honey." She smiled up at her husband.

Mr. Marcus sat on Belinda's opposite side. "Did your dad finally tell you what had happened?"

"Yes, sir."

Mr. Marcus smiled at me. "I haven't been sir for a long time, son. Call me Brian."

"Ye - um - okay, Brian."

He laughed. "Your grandfather did a thorough job, I see, drilling the 'ma'ams' and 'sirs' into you."

"Did you know him?"

"Briefly. Is he still living?"

"Yes, si - um - he is. He's in assisted living near Camp Lejeune. He just turned ninety."

"That's marvelous." Belinda laid her left hand on mine and gave it a gentle squeeze. "I can't tell you how glad I am to see you. Your dad - it was so hard for him. He missed your mom so much. It was too painful for him to keep seeing us, so we kept our distance at his request - but I missed you and your brothers terribly. How are they?"

"They're great. Jeff's a veterinarian here in town, married with two boys. Kevin's a homicide detective in Los Angeles."

Belinda's eyes widened and Brian laughed. "That fits. He was a feisty little fella."

I grinned. "He still is."

"And what about you?"

I gave them the details of my education and employment. Brian said, "Impressive! I'm pleased to know you've all turned out so well."

"Thank you, si - um - Brian."

He laughed. "If it's that much of a struggle to stop saying 'sir,' I guess I can stand hearing it occasionally."

I smiled at him. "Thanks."

Belinda had noticed the ring on my right hand. She asked, "Are you married?"

"No, ma'am. I'm engaged, though."

Belinda said, "Oh, that's wonderful. Who's the lucky girl?"

I bit my lip. This happy reunion might be about to end. "Um - it's a lucky guy."

Brian looked shocked but recovered quickly. "Well. Congratulations."

Not full-throated acceptance, but at least he hadn't thrown me off his property. Belinda patted my hand again. "What's his name?"

"Pete Ferguson. He's a professor of psychology at Santa Monica College."

I'd finished my tea; Brian took my glass and set it on the table. "You must have been surprised to get a copy of Barkley's will."

"Yes, sir. We had no idea who he was."

"Our son and daughter knew who the Barkleys were. But we had no idea he left his estate to all of you."

I said, "The obituary stated that Barkley had no survivors, but Kevin found out that his son is still in Folsom Prison."

Brian said, "From what we heard, Barkley completely disowned his son after his sentencing."

"Dad said that Barkley paid for the best attorneys and everything for the trial. Why would he then turn on his son, after making such an effort to support him?"

Brian shook his head. "I don't know. Barkley did have to pay millions of dollars to the family of the son's girlfriend after they won a civil suit against him. Maybe it was a financial decision."

If Barkley had paid millions to the girlfriend's family, there might not be a lot left for the rest of us. Belinda said, "That poor girl. That was the most devastating part of the trial, when her parents brought her in for their testimony. Barkley's entire demeanor changed after that."

Brian said, "Josh tells us that he's going to a meeting on Monday at the lawyer's office."

I wondered if Josh had received the same letter I had yesterday, but I didn't want to ask for fear of upsetting Belinda. "Yes, sir. Kevin and I asked our attorney to set that up. We want to get some of these questions answered."

Belinda smiled. "That's wonderful. And you'll get to meet Josh. He's a couple of years older than you."

I said, "Have you stayed in touch with your other friend? Marie?"

Belinda's expression grew fond. "Yes. Marie became my best friend. We already lived next door to each other on base, and we'd both been through so much - it drew us together. We kept each other going." She moved her left arm in a semi-gesture toward her wheelchair. "The one good thing about my injury was that I wasn't in pain. Marie suffered terribly."

"Dad said she almost bled to death."

"Yes. She had compound fractures of both femurs. It took multiple surgeries and years of rehabilitation." Belinda closed her eyes.

We had to get off the subject of injuries. I said, "The Crabtrees went back east?"

"Yes." Belinda brightened again. "Rick was transferred to Quantico about four years after the accident and then retired to Atlanta. We still talk on the phone at least twice a week. She has a son in Massachusetts and a daughter in Florida."

"What about Tracy's kids?"

"Tony - Tracy's husband - remarried about a year after the accident, another friend whose husband had been killed in Vietnam. I kept up with them until the kids were in high school, then they divorced and I lost track."

Brian held Belinda's glass for her to take another drink. "This will business is hard to get a handle on."

I shook my head. "Why would Barkley leave money to us? If he really wanted to help us, it looks like he would have established college scholarships or something, not waited until we were grown."

Brian said, "Maybe there's not that much money left."

"That's what my brother Jeff suspects. What about the last name on the list? Jennelle Shifflett?"

Belinda said, "That's a mystery to us. She wasn't involved in the accident case."

Brian said, "I don't remember anyone at Pendleton with that last name when we were all there."

I said, "Maybe she's an illegitimate child of old man Barkley."

Brian huffed a laugh. "Maybe so."

Belinda frowned. "Enough talk about the Barkleys. You'd like to hear about your mom, wouldn't you?"

"Yes, please."

Her expression softened. "Your mom was amazing. She was the youngest of our group but the most accomplished by far. Tracy was also a nurse but wasn't in the military and didn't work after her children were born. Marie and I were never anything but housewives."

Brian said, "Your dad was also the only one of the husbands who'd seen combat. Rick Crabtree and I were stateside during Vietnam and Tony Jemison didn't join until the war was over. Dave and Julie were a special couple."

I said, "Dad has a bunch of old home movies, so I know how she looked and sounded. I get the impression she was pretty funny."

"Oh, my, yes." Belinda laughed lightly. "Julie was a card. And boy, you always knew where you stood with her. We teased her when she was having her kids. We always told her she must be descended from women who gave birth in the fields and went right back to work. I never saw anyone with easier pregnancies."

Brian asked, "Can I get you some more tea?"

"Oh, no, thank you." I checked my watch. "I told my dad I'd be home for lunch, so I'd better get going. But I'm so glad I came."

Belinda reached out and gently squeezed my hand again. "Please come back. Anytime."

Brian and I stood as Pink Scrubs came back onto the patio. "Do you need anything before I go, Mrs. Marcus?"

"No, Francesca, thank you."

"Yes, ma'am. I'll see you tomorrow." She smiled at me again and went back into the house.

I said goodbye to Belinda, and Brian walked me to the top of the driveway. "Please say hello to your dad and Charlie Fortner. They were two of my finest Marines."

"Yes, sir. Dad will be glad to know that Belinda is doing so well."

Brian smiled, but it was tinged with sadness. "She's come a long way. She was so depressed when she got out of rehab. I didn't know what to do." He waved goodbye to Pink Scrubs - Francesca - as she got into a car that had pulled up to the end of the driveway; Francesca and the driver both waved back.

I said, "Who could blame her? But she got past it."

"She did." He smiled again, happier this time. "About a year after she was home, it was as if an internal switch flipped. One day she just decided to make the best of it."

I said, "She's an inspiration."

"She is." Brian shook my hand. "Tell your dad to call me sometime."

"Yes, sir. Thank you."

When I pulled to the curb in front of Dad's house, he and Pete were on the front porch, drinking water and chatting. I said, "What are you all doing out here?"

Dad said, "I'm on the neighborhood watch. So I'm watching. How are Brian and Belinda?"

"Brian is fine. He said to tell you and Mr. Fortner hello."

Dad nodded. "He was several steps above us in the command, but he was a decent guy. What about Belinda?"

"She looks - good, considering her situation. She can move her left shoulder and use her hand well enough to steer her wheelchair, although she can't hold a glass of tea or anything like that. She's a pretty lady. They have a nice cottage, completely adapted for a wheelchair."

"Brian must have help. He wouldn't be able to do it all himself."

"He does. I met the caretaker."

"Did Belinda say anything about Marie Crabtree?"

"Yes, they've stayed in close touch. They talk a couple of times a week."

Dad nodded. "They were best friends before the accident. I'm glad that didn't change."

Pete stood. "Dave, do you have sandwich stuff? I'll make sandwiches, and we can eat out here."

"I think so. You know where everything is?"

"Yes, sir." He went inside.

Dad grinned at me. "He's very domestic."

"And he came that way. I didn't have to train him at all."

That night in bed, Pete asked, "Did you learn anything about your mom?"

"Nothing that I didn't already know. Belinda seemed to admire her."

"From everything I've heard, she was an admirable woman." Pete wound his fingers through mine. "Like her sons."

I chuckled. "Yeah, that's me. Admirable."

"You are. You're very impressive." Pete rubbed my shoulder. "Did you like them?"

"Yeah. They're pleasant people. They've made the best of a bad situation. That's admirable too."

"Indeed." Pete yawned against the top of my head. "G'night."

Sunday, April 5

True to his word, Dad took advantage of having Pete and me available and put us to work. In the morning, we worked in the garden; after lunch we helped Dad do some spring cleaning in the kitchen, emptying cabinets and the fridge, washing all the surfaces and tossing expired food. Dad returned the last can to the pantry as I stacked the final plates on the shelves.

Dad said, "Whew. Great job, guys. This would have taken me all day on my own."

I said, "Happy to oblige. You can pay us in beer."

We carried our beer bottles out to the back yard and grabbed lawn chairs. Dad asked, "How's the wedding planning coming?"

Pete and I looked at each other and laughed. I said, "There's not much to plan."

"Do you have your plane tickets yet?"

Pete said, "Yeah. We fly out the evening of the wedding."

We were taking a three-week honeymoon to Scotland and England. While there, I'd be presenting at a history conference with Fiona Mackenzie, the archivist at the University of Edinburgh. We were going to spend most of the rest of the time in the Hebrides, exploring Pete's ancestry in more detail, and hiking the Hadrian's Wall path.

I said, "If this will turns out to be valid and there's a good chunk of money involved, I'm going to upgrade us to first class."

"Nice." My dad stretched his legs. "Pete, is your dad going to be able to walk up the mountain?"

Pete's face clouded. "I don't think so. He's walking okay on flat surfaces, but Chris says he gets tired after about a half mile. He hasn't been climbing hills."

Pete's dad had suffered a major heart attack five months ago. After two weeks of hospitalization and a month of cardiac rehab, he'd moved to the guest house on Pete's sister's ranch. He'd continued rehab but had lost a lot of heart function in the attack and hadn't progressed as quickly as he'd hoped.

I said, "We can get married in Neil's back yard. That way your dad can be there."

"*No.*" Pete was adamant. "Eagle Rock is our spot. We met there, we got engaged there, we're gonna get married there. I wish my dad could be there, but I wish your mom could be there too. Circumstances don't allow either of those things."

Dad said, "What does Jack say about it?"

Pete snorted softly. "He said, 'I wasn't at Chris's or Steve's weddings either. Seems to be a tradition that I miss my kids' weddings. At least I'll be at your reception.'"

I said, "I know why he wasn't at Chris and Andy's wedding, but why did he miss Steve's?"

"We all missed Steve's. He and Meredith eloped because her family didn't want her to marry a white guy."

"Ah." Steve's ex-wife was Navajo. "Did they ever warm up to him?"

Pete chuckled. "He told me a while ago that her parents *really* don't like the guy she's been seeing most recently. They even made a comment like, 'You left that smart engineer for this?' And the guy's Native American."

Dad and I laughed. Dad said, "Navajo?"

"No, Apache."

I said, "You all have a Cahuilla great-grandmother. I guess that wasn't enough for Meredith's parents?"

Dad said, "Sounds like they're coming around to the idea."

Pete said, "It might not be too late. Every time I talk to Steve, he's recently seen Meredith. Seems like she's been spending a lot of time in Las Cruces on business."

That night in bed, I said, "Is it truly okay with you that your dad won't be at the wedding? 'Cause if it's not, we can change the location."

He rolled up on his side to face me. "You'd do that for me, wouldn't you?"

"Of course I would."

He smiled and reached out to stroke my face. "Think of it this way. I had to weigh the fact of my dad not being able to come to the wedding against us not being able to get married where and how we want. Which of those do *you* think is more important to me?"

"I get that, but…"

He stopped me with a finger against my lips. "You are more important to me. Our marriage is the *most* important thing to me. I want it to begin exactly the way we've imagined it. Besides - I really don't think Dad is overwhelmingly disappointed."

"Okay. If you're sure."

"I'm *positive.*"

"Are you just as positive that you want to get married on your birthday?"

Thanks to a bit of light filtering through the blinds from the streetlight outside, I could see Pete's expression of curiosity. "Why wouldn't I be?"

"Because then we don't ever get to just celebrate your birthday. It's like being born on Christmas."

He grinned. "Listen, I can't think of a better birthday present for me than getting to marry you. And this way, I'll never forget our anniversary."

"Like you ever would anyway." I ran a finger down the center of his chest. "Is it because you're turning forty?"

I thought I might have hit on something; his expression shifted slightly. "Why would it be?"

"Turning forty is a big deal for some guys. Midlife crises have been known to occur. You haven't said anything about being forty at all. It occurred to me that if you were trying to avoid thinking about turning forty, getting married on that day would help put it out of your mind."

He was quiet for a minute then said, "Sometimes you're too smart for your own good."

"So I'm your midlife crisis?"

That made him laugh, and he pulled me against him. "I'll show you midlife crisis…"

Monday, April 6

That night, I dreamed that Pete surprised me on our wedding day with a shiny red sports car.

Midlife crisis, indeed.

Our appointment at Smith, Hendrickson, Delio and Franklin wasn't until noon, so I was surprised when Kevin knocked on Dad's door at 10:00. I said, "You're early."

"Yeah. Wanted a few minutes to chill. Traffic was a bitch."

Kevin wasn't in a good mood. He greeted Dad, got a Coke from the fridge, and plopped onto the sofa in the living room. Pete, Dad and I all trailed in after him and watched as he drained half the Coke. He lowered the bottle and noticed all of us looking at him. "What?"

Dad said, "What's wrong?"

Kevin waved a hand in disgust. "Abby picked a fight this morning. As usual."

I said, "About what?"

"She didn't want me to come down here."

Pete asked, "Why?"

"I don't know. She couldn't articulate it in a way that made any sense to me. She 'sort of has a bad feeling' about the money." Kevin's air quotes - made with his middle fingers - expressed his displeasure.

Pete looked puzzled. "Why?"

"She can't explain it."

Dad asked, "How are things?"

"Honestly? Not good. She's pestering me to quit the force. She wants to spend Thanksgiving *and* Christmas with her family *again* this year. She's stirring up an argument every day about something or other, and I'm over it."

Pete said, "Is she doing it on purpose?"

"Beats the hell out of me. There's no logic in that. If we break up, she can't afford the house on her own. I don't know what she's thinking."

Dad said, "Do you think it's heading for a breakup?"

Kevin bit his lip. "I don't know. I don't want to split up. But…" He pinched the bridge of his nose, grimacing. "I let her explain her position, I'm trying to do what she wants, but it's nearly impossible. Her latest thing is that she's decided she doesn't like Jon and Liz."

I said, "Why the hell now? You and Jon have been partners for a year and a half."

"I don't know. I really don't." Kevin sighed and stood up. "Let me hit the head, and we'd better get going."

Kevin and I picked up Jeff at his office, where he'd had a couple of early-morning surgeries to do. We had both worn sport coats and ties; Jeff was in his work clothes, jeans and a polo shirt with "Miracosta Animal Hospital" embroidered on it. I didn't say anything, but Kevin looked him up and down. "A little casual for a meeting downtown, aren't you?"

Jeff glared at Kevin. "I didn't have time to change."

I said, "At least he wiped off all the animal hair."

The offices of Smith, Henderson, Delio and Franklin occupied the entire top floor of one of San Diego's downtown high-rises. When we stepped off the elevator, it was like walking into a museum. The floors were black marble covered with lush Oriental rugs; Impressionist art lined the walls. The waiting room was furnished with overstuffed armchairs and end tables with vases of fresh-cut flowers.

The receptionist's desk was made of the same marble as the floor. A young guy in an expensive charcoal suit and striped tie was manning the desk. He looked up at us and my gaydar pinged, but he made no expression that could be considered the least bit flirtatious. "May I help you?"

I gave him our names. "We have an appointment with Mr. Smith."

"Yes. We're waiting for two more. Please have a seat."

I sat. Jeff went to the windows and studied the view of the bay; Kevin looked at the art. Less than a minute later, the elevator doors opened, and two guys stepped out. One was about my age, dressed in a suit and tie. The other was a few years older, in jeans, a t-shirt and a windbreaker.

The guy in the suit had a strong resemblance to Brian Marcus. He eyed us curiously for a second then said, "Are you the Brodies?"

I said, "Yes. Are you Josh Marcus?"

"Yeah."

"I'm Jamie." Josh and I shook hands.

The guy in jeans said, "We're all here for the same thing."

Josh turned to him. "Who are you?"

Jeff said, "Drew Jemison."

I shot Jeff a look. *How did he know that?* Drew's mouth curved into a half-smile. "Hi, Jeff. I wondered if you'd remember."

Remember what? Jeff said, "Just barely. I remember the green Nerf football."

Drew laughed. Kevin and I gave each other a look - *WTF?* But that would have to wait. I said, "Do you all live in the area?"

Josh said, "I live in LA now. My mother said you do, too. She enjoyed her visit with you on Saturday."

"So did I. What part of LA?"

"Marina Del Rey."

Fancy. I said, "Are you local, Drew?"

Drew looked a little uncomfortable. "Yeah." He didn't elaborate.

The receptionist had a brief conversation with someone via intercom. Shortly thereafter, a door opened in the wall, and a woman in a navy suit gave us a professional smile. "Come with me please, gentlemen."

We followed her into a short hallway which opened into another reception area, similar to the first but not quite as large. The woman didn't introduce herself. "Please have a seat. Mr. Smith's assistant will be with you shortly."

In two or three more minutes, another door opened and a familiar face appeared. Michelle Richardson. She gave us another professional smile, but it was much warmer than the others we'd seen. "This way, please."

I said, "Thank you for arranging this."

She gave me a nod. "Glad to do it."

We walked into another hallway, longer, with several doors leading from it. One opened into a good-sized library, where a couple of young people in suits were working. At the end of the hall, we were escorted through a final door.

I had to check my initial reaction, which was to whistle in disbelief. I'd been in the office of the chancellor of UCLA, and this office put the chancellor's to shame. The room was huge, with a wall of windows looking out at the bay. The walls here were lined in dark wood paneling.

At the far end of the office, behind an enormous desk, a distinguished-looking, silver-haired man in an expensive suit stood and walked around to greet us. "Gentlemen, welcome. I'm Gordon Smith."

We introduced ourselves. Smith indicated a grouping of armchairs at the far end of the office. "Please, have a seat. Can I get any of you something to drink?"

We all refused. Smith sat in the remaining chair and gave us a practiced, professional smile. "It's perfectly natural that you gentlemen should have questions. How can I help you?"

We all glanced at each other for a second, then Kevin said, "Why? After Barkley defended his son so vigorously at trial, why leave us the estate?"

Smith sighed. "Randall - as so many of us do - began rethinking his life as he aged and began to face his own mortality. He had regrets. He came to believe that he had been responsible for his son's actions, because of the lenient way in which he'd raised Gavin. He became more and more burdened by guilt - consumed by it, in all honesty. He asked me five years ago to find each of you, to discover what circumstances you were living in. When I reported back to him, he told me that he wanted to rewrite his will to divide his estate among you." He gave us a wry smile. "I tried to talk him out of it. From what I'd learned about you, I feared that a sudden inheritance from a man that you'd probably been raised to hate might be - disruptive."

I said, "We weren't raised to hate him. We'd never heard of him."

Drew remained silent. Josh said, "I knew who he was."

Smith nodded. "However, Randall was insistent that the nine of you receive the inheritance. So I drew up the papers."

Kevin said, "What about his son?"

Smith looked pained. "Randall and his son had ceased all contact. Gavin wanted to be left alone to serve his sentence in peace, and Randall had nothing left to say to Gavin. They haven't spoken since Randall told Gavin of his mother's passing."

Josh said, "Randall Senior has essentially disowned his son. Was that his intention?"

"Yes. Randall's words to me were that all of you had to make your own way in the world, and now it was Gavin's turn."

Drew said, "How much money are we talking about?"

Smith smiled, as if he'd been anticipating the question. "I received the final figures today, as the closing for the sale of Randall's home took place last week. The value of the estate is $683 million. Give or take a few cents."

Jeff turned pale. Kevin looked stunned. I sucked in a breath. Barkley hadn't spent his fortune; he'd added to it.

Drew's eyes widened. "Holy fucking *shit*."

A slight twitch of disapproval flickered across Smith's face, so quickly I almost missed it. Josh said, "Estate taxes will take nearly half of that."

His tone was a bit smarmy. My instantaneous reaction was, *Suck up.* Gordon Smith seemed pleased. "Divided ten ways, after taxes, each of you should be left with roughly thirty-eight million dollars."

Drew laughed harshly. "I'll take it."

Jeff said, "What if we don't want it?"

We all stared at him. Kevin said, "What are you talking about?"

Jeff's face was stony. "This is blood money. Paying us off for the death of our mothers just to ease his own conscience. What if I want to refuse it?"

Drew was looking at Jeff like he was deranged. I thought he was deranged myself. Josh said, "Seriously? Who turns down thirty-eight million?"

I said, "He's not turning it down."

Jeff shot me a look. "Maybe I am."

Kevin was shaking his head. Smith looked shocked. "Of course that would be your decision. But I'd consider that very, very carefully."

Josh said, "If he drops out, is it divided nine ways?"

Smith cleared his throat. "Yes."

Silence reigned for a moment. Kevin said, "He doesn't have to give you his final decision today, does he?"

"No. The money will be available for distribution in two weeks. We will need your decision by then."

Drew stood. "We done here?"

Smith had an expression of distaste, as if he'd never met anyone quite so rude, but he maintained his calm demeanor. "If you have no further questions, yes."

"Awesome. Thanks." Drew shot us a grin and disappeared out the door.

Smith looked after him for a minute, then turned back to us. "If you were my clients, I would advise each of you to retain an attorney familiar with estate law and a certified financial planner who understands the tax ramifications of an inheritance."

Josh said, "Would it be a conflict of interest for you to represent us?"

Definitely a suck up. Smith smiled at Josh. "Unfortunately, yes. If you would like, I can recommend several experienced attorneys." He glanced at us, including us in his offer.

Kevin said, "We already have a lawyer. But thank you."

Smith stood. "If you have any further questions, please contact us. My paralegal will be happy to address any issues."

I said, "I do have one other question. Who is Jennelle Shifflett?"

Smith's smoothly professional expression didn't waver, but something disquieting flickered in his eyes. "Ms. Shifflett is an old friend of the Barkley family."

Hm. Maybe she *was* Barkley's illegitimate daughter. Or mistress. I cocked an eyebrow at Smith, and he narrowed his eyes at me.

Interesting.

Kevin stood. "We appreciate your time, sir. Thank you."

Smith looked relieved. "You are quite welcome."

We rode the elevator to the ground floor with Josh Marcus. We were all silent, occupied with our own thoughts. My thoughts were that Jeff must have lost his mind. Surely Kevin and I could talk him out of turning down the money.

When we walked out of the building Josh turned to us. "I'm going to see my parents. It was good to meet you."

Kevin said, "You too."

We watched him walk away, then turned and went to Kevin's car. I said, "Jeff?"

His face was a mask. "Wait until we get home."

We walked into Jeff's cool, empty house. Val and the boys were out; Val was probably picking Gabe up from school. I hung my jacket on a chair, took off my tie, tossed it on the kitchen table and turned to face Jeff. "What the hell is the matter with you?"

Jeff had stopped at the fridge to get a beer; now he smacked it down on the counter and whirled to face me. "What the hell is the matter with you two? I can't believe you're taking blood money."

"*Blood* money? Isn't that a little dramatic?"

Jeff took a step closer to me. "I'll tell you what's dramatic. When that asshole's kid killed our mom, that asshole tried to get him off. And now he's trying to buy his way into heaven or something. It sounds like a bad movie. I'm not having anything to do with it. And I can't believe you would even consider it."

"Jeff. You've got two kids, a mortgage on this place, a mortgage on your practice… You and Ben can't hire a third vet because you can't afford it, so you work more than you have to, so you don't have enough time with your family. You could solve all those problems. Why would you *not* do that?"

Jeff edged even closer to me. "Don't you try to tell me *anything* about how I take care of my family. What the fuck would *you* know about taking care of a family?"

I could see in Jeff's face that he wanted to take the words back as soon as he'd said them. But it was too late. They were already lodged in my heart, the quiver on the arrow still vibrating. I backed away from him, trying to restrain my hurt and anger. Jeff took a step toward me. "Jamie…"

I threw up my hands to stop him, but Kevin was there first, planting his hand in the center of Jeff's chest. "Let him go."

I turned and stalked out of the house, moving toward the barn. The big barn doors were closed. I went around to the back, where I found a convenient stack of straw bales, and slugged the one at eye level.

I kept punching the straw until I'd dismantled an entire bale; the one above it toppled over, landing at my feet. I dropped onto it. Ralphie, Jeff and Val's big yellow Lab, trotted up beside me to be petted. I stroked his soft head and whispered, "Hey, Ralphie."

Ralphie responded by putting his paw on my knee and licking my face. I put up my hand to ward off his sloppy doggy kisses - and discovered that he was licking tears from my face. I hadn't even realized I was crying.

I wondered what was going on in the house. I was too far away to hear anything. I leaned back against the barn wall and looked at the pasture, where Val's goats were munching grass. I was short of breath, and I'd left my inhaler in my jacket pocket - which was now hanging over the back of a chair in Jeff's kitchen.

My brothers had always been my staunchest defenders. I'd thought they'd been equal in that. Now I had to wonder. Jeff had never, ever said anything to me like that before. I'd never seen the slightest indication that he thought less of me because I was gay.

Now I had.

Another consequence of Randall Barkley's bequest.

I took a deep breath - or tried to. I really needed my inhaler. I stood up and wiped my face on my shirtsleeve, hoping I didn't look too awful. I went back around the barn, Ralphie on my heels, and approached the house. I could see Val, Colin and Gabe on the patio - and as I got closer, I could hear the raised voices from the house.

Jeff and Kevin were yelling at each other.

Val's face was tight. Colin's was pale, his eyes wide. Gabe jumped up from where he'd been huddled against his mom and ran to me, throwing his arms around my waist. "Why is Daddy yelling?"

Val said, "Good question. What's going on?"

I said, "Jeff's turning down the money."

"He's *what??*"

I shook my head. "He'll have to tell you why."

'He'd damn well *better* tell me why." Val indicated the house with her head. "Is that what they're - discussing?"

"I don't think so." I gave Gabe a hug. "Hey, Gabers, can you do me a big favor? I need my inhaler, and it's in my jacket, hanging on a chair in the kitchen. Can you get my jacket for me?"

Gabe brightened, having a task to fulfill. "Sure, Uncle Jamie." He ran to the kitchen door and slipped inside.

The shouting stopped.

A minute later Gabe reappeared, with Kevin behind him. Kevin had my jacket and tie, and he handed them to me. I dug into my pocket, found my inhaler and took a puff. Then a couple of deep breaths. "That's better."

Val said, "Kevin. What the hell?"

Kevin shook his head. He was furious, I could tell, but he was in professional cop mode, holding his temper back. "I'd give him a minute."

Val looked back and forth between us. "I guess you're not staying for dinner."

Kevin barked a laugh. "No."

Val was smart, and she knew us all well enough to figure out what might have happened. She hugged me tightly and whispered in my ear, "Whatever he said, he didn't mean it."

I hugged back, then gave her a wan smile. "I think he did."

When Val had stood, Kevin had sat down beside Colin and had his arm around him, talking softly to him. He said to me, "Ready to go?"

"Yeah."

Kevin hugged Val too. I said, "We'll see you soon."

"Okay."

We went to the car. I said, "You okay to drive?"

"Sure. I'm used to driving while pissed."

We got to the end of the driveway and Kevin stopped. "Are you all right?"

"The inhaler's doing its job."

"That's not what I meant."

I couldn't look at him. I said weakly, "I always thought he was on my side."

Kevin shook his head. "He says he didn't mean it like it sounded."

"That doesn't make it okay."

"I told him that."

We drove in silence for a minute. I said, "What the fuck is Jeff thinking? It's as if this will thing has twisted his brain."

Kevin gripped the steering wheel a little tighter. "He thinks that taking the money would be a betrayal of Mom and Dad."

"Dad doesn't feel like that."

"I know. Jeff hasn't even talked to him."

I leaned my head back on the rest. "I've never seen Jeff like this."

"Neither have I."

"Colin and Gabe were scared when they heard you all yelling at each other."

"I'm sorry they had to hear that. I told Colin it was just an argument and for him not to worry. I don't know if he listened."

"Val didn't know that Jeff wants to turn down the money."

"She *didn't?*"

"Nope."

"Well then. Val will unleash the shitstorm."

"What did you say to him?"

"About the money, that he was being a selfish asshole and he needed to think of his wife and kids, not his own absurdly emotional reaction to this situation. About you, that I was disappointed in him. That's when he told me what he'd meant by what he'd said."

"Which was?"

"That you have no idea what it's like to bear the responsibility for a family and a business and employees. He included me in that too."

"Does he realize how it sounded to me?"

Kevin sighed. "Not fully. I tried to school him on that. I'm not sure how successful I was."

We got to Dad's a few minutes later; Kevin dropped me at the front door. "I've gotta get back to LA. I'll talk to you later."

"Okay." I punched him gently in the shoulder. "Thanks for sticking up for me."

He started to punch me back, then remembered my shoulder injury and fake-punched my jaw instead. "Always, short stuff."

When I opened the door, the house smelled divine. Vegetable soup, I thought. Dad was nowhere to be seen. Pete had brought work with him; he was on the sofa, surrounded by books, making notes. His bright smile when he saw me began to fade as he took me in. "Hey, hon. How'd it go?"

I tossed my jacket and tie on an armchair and dropped down beside Pete. "The lawyer's office was cordial and interesting. A little weird. The aftermath, not so much. Where's Dad?"

"He just left for the grocery store." Pete frowned. "What happened?"

As I recounted the day's events, Pete's frown changed to an expression of increasing disbelief. When I said "six hundred and eighty-three million," his jaw dropped. When I told him that Jeff had tried to turn down the money, he made a "pah" sound. "Is he *nuts?*"

I tried to make light of it. "Won't they take away your psychologist's license for calling someone nuts?"

"In this case, every psychologist in the state would agree with me."

"That's not all." I told Pete about the conversation at Jeff's house.

He pressed his lips into a thin line. "How *dare* he. What did you do?"

"I went behind the barn and demolished a bale of straw. Then Val came home – she didn't know that Jeff wanted to turn down the money."

"Wow. How to alienate your entire family in a few short hours."

"Tell me about it." I scrubbed my hands through my hair. "I've never seen him like this."

"What are you going to do?"

"For now? Nothing. Wait and see what happens." I smiled at him, although it was a weak effort. "I'm going to change clothes."

"Okay." Pete stood and hugged me, holding me for a minute, then gave me a quick kiss. "When your dad gets back, we'll eat."

When Dad pulled into the driveway, I went out to help with the groceries. He said, "I hear you've had an interesting day."

I barked a laugh. "You could say that. Who did you talk to?"

"Val. I called her to find out if I'd be feeding Colin tomorrow, and she gave me a brief rundown. Let me tell you a couple of things."

"Sure, okay."

We'd made it to the kitchen, and Dad set his bags on the table, then turned to me. "First, and most importantly, let me reassure you that I have no problem with you taking Randall Barkley's money. None *whatsoever*. I don't know where Jeff has gotten this idea that taking the money would somehow be disloyal to your mom and me. As far as I'm concerned, better you should have it than anyone else. It's the *least* Barkley could do."

"Okay. I was starting to wonder."

"Well, don't. Second, what Jeff said to you was thoughtless, and he owes you an apology." Dad's tone gentled. "You and Kevin have your mom's temper. Yell, get it out in the open, then get over it and move on. Jeff's always been one to hold it in until it boils over. I guess he gets that from me, but he's got a much worse case of it. And it sure seems to me like he's holding something in that's about to boil over."

I said sadly, "I always thought he was on my side."

My dad sighed. "He is on your side, sport. I guarantee you he's eating himself up inside over what he said to you."

"It hurt."

"Of course it did. But I truly don't believe he meant it in a homophobic sense. He would have said the same thing to Kevin in similar circumstances. He's always seen himself as the responsible family man when compared to the two of you."

"The irresponsible little brothers."

"Exactly. I know it'll be hard to forgive him, but I hope you can."

"I can. Forgetting is something else."

"Sure. But I think - I hope - he'll learn some valuable things about himself from this episode."

Pete and I didn't talk much on the drive home. Pete drove and I replayed the events of the weekend in my head, thinking about what Jeff had said, thinking about the contrasts between scruffy Drew Jemison and business-like Josh Marcus. I wondered how the Crabtree kids had turned out.

And I wanted to know more about Jennelle Shifflett.

And a green Nerf football.

I was still brooding somewhat in the evening, but Pete did a good job of distracting me in the shower. Afterward, we curled up in bed together, not quite ready to sleep. Pete said, "What's your wish list?"

"For the money? The first thing I'm going to do is stop teaching these extra history classes."

"*Good.* I was hoping you'd say that."

"Do you want a new Jeep?"

He laughed. "Not really. Are you sure you don't want a car?"

"I'm sure. You know what I think would be a good idea, though? A piece of property, somewhere outside the earthquake zone."

"Ah, that is a good idea. Where?"

"What about New Mexico? Close to Steve, not far from the rest of your family and our marriage would be recognized."

Pete smiled. "Would you want to live in Alamogordo?"

"Why not? That way Steve can keep an eye on the place when we're not there. And we already know other people there - Brian Cochrane, Russell and Mandy McCarthy."

"Would you want to be that far from your family?"

I'd thought about that. "I don't see us living there full time. At least not yet. It would be more of a retreat. Our families could join us there, or use it for their own vacations."

"We could build somewhere in San Diego County."

"And pay California taxes and impact fees? No. And I refuse to live in Arizona."

Pete chuckled. "Good point."

"In Alamogordo, we're with Steve and we're a tad closer to the rest of your family. And we'll still be here most of the time, close to my family. The best of both worlds."

"Okay." Pete mused. "If we built rather than bought, we could make it as self-sufficient as possible."

"Oh, that's a good idea. Solar from the start."

"Yep. Okay, a second home is on the list. What else?"

I said, "Let's remodel both bathrooms here. We've been talking about it, now we can go ahead."

"Sounds good. What else?"

I remembered my earthquake dream. "We need a tent."

Pete squinted at me in disbelief. "Huh?"

"Never mind. I think I want to sock the rest of it someplace safe in case one of us gets laid off or sick or something."

Pete said, "We could quit our jobs and move to Scotland."

I couldn't see his facial expression in the dark. "Are you *serious?*"

"No. Maybe." His voice was full of wonder. "*Anything* is possible now."

I sighed. "We need some financial advice."

Tuesday, April 7

The next morning when I got on the bus, I checked email on my phone - and saw a message from Jeff.

The subject line was *I am so, so, so, sorry*. He'd sent it at 2:00 am. I clicked it open.

Hey Jamie,

I wanted to call you tonight but Val said it was too late and I wasn't sure you'd pick up when you saw it was me. I am so sorry for what I said. I didn't mean it the way it sounded. I just meant you didn't have kids so you didn't know what that was like. It didn't have anything to do with you being gay. I wanted to take the words back as soon as I saw the look on your face, because I realized how you were taking it.

I'm an idiot.

I know you and Pete are a family, even if it's just the two of you. We're all family. It's just that you and Pete have no debt, no dependents, two incomes - you don't have the same burden of responsibility that I do. But that's not an excuse.

Like I said, I'm an idiot.

I don't know what's wrong with me. This will thing has just made me crazy. I just felt like having anything to do with the Barkleys was wrong. It felt so WRONG. I don't know why. I talked to Dad last night for a long time and he convinced me that I'm wrong about that. He wants us to have the money.

I think part of it was that I felt like Barkley was buying us off, implying that the money would make up for us not having our mom. And it pissed me off because nothing can make up for that. I watch Val with our boys and I wonder how our lives would have been different if we'd been raised by Mom instead of Sarge. I know it's ridiculous because there's not a thing I can do about it but I can't help it. I'd been working on converting more of Dad's old movies recently too so that was probably part of my mindset as well.

None of that is an excuse.

Val was so mad at me. She told me not to come to bed until I'd written this. I've been apologizing to her all night. She kept asking, "What is wrong with you?" and I couldn't answer her.

But she's right. You and Kevin are right. I'm the one who needs the money the most, with the practice and the farm and the kids. I'm going to call the attorney's office in the morning and tell them to leave me on the list.

I want to get with you and Kevin and talk about setting something up for Dad once we get the money. I don't know if Mel has mentioned this but it occurred to me that we all need to talk to Lauren.

Lauren Fortner was Ali's sister. She'd been in Jeff's class from grade school on. They had been - and still were - good friends, and Lauren was Jeff's accountant.

You know she's a CPA and a certified financial planner and her office is here in Oceanside. Between Lauren and Mel we need to set things up right so everything is protected.

But we can talk about that later.

Jamie, I have always been so proud to be your big brother. You and Kevin both, but especially you. Everything you've accomplished, how you've lived your life with such integrity.

Please forgive me.

I'll call you tomorrow - please talk to me.

Love you,
Jeff

I sniffed a little and put my phone away - then pulled it back out and texted him. *Got your email. Love you too. Call me this evening.*

He answered immediately. *I will. Thank you. Have a good day.*

I sent him a smiley face, put my phone away again and sighed, leaning back against the bus seat.

I had a hundred things to do to compensate for being gone yesterday, so I didn't get a chance to talk to Liz until we got to the reference desk. The first thing she said was, under her breath, "How much?"

"After taxes, thirty-eight."

"*Million?*"

"Yep."

She stared at me for a second then whispered, "Jesus, Mary and *Joseph*."

Pretty funny, coming from a Buddhist. I said, "Don't tell anyone here."

She made the sign of zipping her lips, and we turned to deal with our patrons.

Clinton's word of the day was *slubber*. I said, "Is that related to slobber?"

Liz was reading the definition. "No. It means to perform hastily or carelessly." She frowned. "What's that about?"

I said, "We are not to decide what to do with this money hastily or carelessly."

"Do you have a financial adviser? Because I think the guy my parents use is pretty good." Liz's parents were both physicians.

"We do. Ali's sister, actually. She's a CPA and a financial planner. She's already Jeff's accountant."

"Good." Liz gave me a fierce face. "I don't want you to end up on the streets like some of those lottery winners."

I smiled. "Not gonna happen."

"I'm *serious*."

"So am I."

"I'm going to *scrutinize* you for personality changes."

"Good. That'll be your job. Make sure I'm keeping my head on straight."

A student was approaching. Liz hissed, "If you don't, I'll *knock* you straight."

I clutched my head, Edvard Munch-style. "Nooooooo…"

Liz snickered. The student gave me a curious look. I quickly composed myself. "Sorry. Can I help you?"

Shortly before 5:00, I walked south through campus to the medical office building at UCLA Medical Center to meet Pete at our counselor's office. We'd been seeing Dr. Tania Bibbins, both together and separately, for a couple of years. We'd met our therapeutic goals several months ago and now only saw her once a month, on the first Tuesday, for maintenance purposes.

Dr. Bibbins greeted us with a smile and a mug of tea. "What's been happening?"

We hadn't had much news for her since our engagement in November. Now I said, "You are not going to *believe* this."

She looked askance at me. "Okay…"

I gave her the short version of the inheritance story. When I told her the amount, she gasped - a first, in our experience. "Good *Lord*."

"Right?"

She stared at me for a minute, then turned to Pete. "How do *you* feel about this?"

"I'm astounded. It hasn't sunk in at all."

I said, "It doesn't seem real to me."

Dr. Bibbins had regained her composure. "That's a normal response. Have you discussed yet how you might handle the money?"

I said, "Just briefly. I think we should save most of it."

"Pete, do you agree?"

"We're not going to save all of it. We may build a second home near my brother."

"Do you have a financial adviser?"

"Yes, and an attorney."

"Good." Dr. Bibbins set her tea aside. "Sudden riches can put strain on a relationship. You two are skilled at keeping the lines of communication open, but it's particularly important that you do that now."

I said, "We will."

"I would also recommend that you not stop working, at least for a year. If at all. One of the first things that many lottery winners do is quit their jobs. That often turns out to be a mistake. Work gives us structure and purpose. Money does not."

Pete said, "Agreed."

Dr. Bibbins said, "How are your brothers handling this?"

I grimaced. "Not quite as smoothly." I filled her in on Jeff's and Abby's reactions.

She frowned. "How do you feel about your brother's apology?"

"I can understand where he's coming from, I guess."

"It's as important for him to understand your reaction as it is for you to understand his." Dr. Bibbins crossed her arms. "Satisfy yourself that he realizes the implications of his words."

"I will."

Dr. Bibbins nodded. "Good. If any inheritance-related issues arise for you two as a couple, we can increase the frequency of our sessions to address those." She turned to a blank page in her notebook. "What I'd like you to create before our next visit is a list of long-term goals. Until now we've focused on short-term goals and compatibility issues. Now that you have the means to achieve whatever long-term goals you'd like, we should discuss what those goals are."

I let Pete read Jeff's email as we were eating dinner. He said, "As apologies go, that's pretty good."

"Yeah. I texted him, told him to call me tonight."

I'd just finished washing dishes when my phone rang. I answered immediately. "Hey."

The relief in Jeff's voice was palpable. "Hey. Thank you for texting me this morning. Thank you for not hating me."

"Jeff. C'mon. I'll never hate you."

"I wasn't sure."

"Are you interested in a teachable moment?"

"Okay…"

I said, "They're called microaggressions. Little slights that happen every day without the people who are doing the slighting realizing it. All minority groups experience it - people of color, LGBT people, even women. When you're at the top of the food chain, so to speak, you've never experienced that."

"Top of the food chain. You mean straight white men."

"Basically, yeah. 'Cause I know it may not look like it from your vantage point, but y'all run the world."

He snorted. "You're right. It sure doesn't look like it from here."

I sighed. "You know how you can make this up to me, if you're interested? Listen to your boys. Teach them what's right and wrong to say to people who aren't like them. Make sure they grow up to be part of the solution."

"I'll do that. God, Jamie, I am so sorry…"

I said, "Stop. You've apologized. Incidentally, that was an excellent idea you had about Lauren. It hadn't occurred to me to talk to her, but she's the perfect person to help us."

"Yes, she is. Maybe on a Saturday after tax season you and Kev can come down and we can all meet with her?"

"Sure. Saturdays are always fine with me. You'll have to check with Kevin about his schedule."

"I will." Jeff hesitated for a minute then asked, "Would you have any interest in going to see Gavin Barkley?"

That shocked me into silence for a moment. "Are you *serious?*"

"Yes. You read his letter. He wants the chance to apologize in person; I want to give it to him. We can go this weekend."

"Um -" I had to admit, I was curious. But... "What difference is this going to make?"

"I don't know. Maybe none. I just want a chance to look the guy in the eye, and I'd rather not go alone."

"I'd rather you didn't go alone, too. You can forget about Kevin."

Jeff made a "pah" sound. "I wasn't even going to ask him. I'll make the arrangements and pay for the hotel room if you'll come with me."

"Are you sure?"

"I'm sure." He barked a laugh. "I'm about to be a millionaire, remember?"

"I remember. Hey, speaking of remembering things - what's with you and Drew Jemison?"

Jeff was silent for a minute. "I'm surprised that I recognized him. I think Tracy used to babysit us when Mom worked. Drew would have been about six."

"What about the football?"

"Drew had a green Nerf football. He'd toss it to me out in their backyard. That's about all I remember of it."

"You weren't even three."

"I know. Some kids' memories go back further than others."

I said softly, "How far do yours go back, Jeff?"

He hesitated. "Not much more than that." I heard Val's voice in the background. "Better go. Love you."

"Love you too."

Pete had been listening to my side of the conversation from the other end of the sofa. He said, "That sounds like it went well."

"Yeah." I sighed and flipped the phone onto the ottoman. "He sounded tired. This is stressing him out."

"It's a stressful situation. You know how many lottery winners end up worse off than they were before they won? It's like

Dr. B. said. Sudden windfalls change everything about your life, including your relationships and your image of yourself."

"Yeah. And this is stirring up Jeff's feelings about Mom, too."

"Sure. Because it's connected." Pete gave me a curious look. "Does he remember her?"

"He's always said he didn't. Why do you ask?"

He shook his head, looking thoughtful. "Just wondered because of his reaction. But it's unlikely, isn't it? He was not even three yet."

"True. But - Jeff knew who Drew Jemison was before Drew introduced himself, and Drew said, 'Hi Jeff, I wondered if you'd remember.'"

"Remember what?"

"Apparently Tracy Jemison babysat us when Mom went back to work. Jeff said he didn't remember much, just a green Nerf football. Why wouldn't he have ever mentioned it?"

Pete huffed a laugh. "Beats me. He's your brother."

"He wants to go see Barkley at Folsom. This Saturday."

Pete grimaced. "What do you hope to accomplish?"

"Jeff says he wants to look him in the eye. I don't want Jeff to go alone."

"It's a long drive just to look at a face."

"I know. Do you think we shouldn't go?"

He shook his head. "It wouldn't be my choice. But you've got to decide."

Saturday, April 12

The rest of the week passed uneventfully. Saturday morning, Pete and I got up early and went for a run, then I packed an overnight bag and quickly did my weekend vacuuming and bathroom cleaning. Jeff was supposed to pick me up at 10:00 for the drive to Folsom.

He was fifteen minutes early. I was rinsing the cleaner from our bathroom sink when the doorbell rang, and I heard Pete greet Jeff. I washed my hands and came halfway downstairs. "You're early."

"I know. Traffic was lighter than I expected."

I finished up quickly, changed from shorts into jeans and a t-shirt and grabbed my bag. Jeff was in the kitchen talking to Pete when I came down. He said, "Ready?"

"Yup." I went to the fridge and took out a bottle of water. Pete walked us to the door and gave me a goodbye hug and kiss. "Text me when you get there."

"I will."

Jeff drove a CR-V, which was several years old. I strapped myself into the passenger seat and said, "You can get a new one of these now if you want."

He started the car and pulled away from the curb. "Maybe. This one still runs fine. What's the best way to the 5 from here?"

I guided Jeff out Wilshire to the 405, and we headed north. Once we were merged into traffic, Jeff said, "Driving in LA always makes me twitch."

I laughed. "You'd get used to it."

"I'm glad I don't have to." He glanced over at me, his expression anxious. "Are we okay?"

More or less. Maybe. "We're fine. Cut it out."

"Okay." He relaxed. "Are you going to get a car?"

"No. I don't want one. In the year and a half since the Bug died, I haven't needed one. What about you?"

"I'll get a new pickup for farm rounds."

Jeff's current pickup truck was a battered Ford F-150 that was at least ten years old. "That's a good idea. You don't want to get stranded out in the boonies because your truck died."

"No. And I'm going to be spending more time out there."

"How so?"

"Ben and Kim came over last night, and we talked about the practice." Ben Khaladjian was Jeff's partner in his veterinary practice; his wife Kim taught high school science. "Ben and I have been dividing all the work evenly between us, but he prefers the small animal stuff, and I'd rather spend the majority of my time with the large animals. So the first thing I'm going to do with the money is pay off the mortgage on the practice, then we can afford to hire a third vet. Ben and the third person will take the office, and I'll take all the farm work."

"What about call? Won't you get out of practice with the small animals?"

"We're going to stop providing emergency service for small animals on weekends and holidays. One of the other practices in town offers twenty-four hour coverage, so we're duplicating services unnecessarily. The third person we hire will have to have large animal experience, and we'll keep rotating call for the large animals."

"And it'll be every third weekend, not every other."

"Right."

"Won't Ben owe you for his part of the mortgage payoff?"

"Yeah. We're gonna treat it like an interest-free loan, from me to him, and he'll gradually pay me off. We're going to manage it through payroll, though, so the only difference will be that part of his share of the income ends up in my check."

"Jeez. Business is complicated. I'm glad I'm a simple employee."

He chuckled. "You gonna remain a simple employee?"

"Yep. I love my job."

"Good." He glanced over. "How's your shoulder?"

"Getting there. I'm still doing my exercises."

"Have you started back to swimming yet?"

"No. I go back to the doctor in a couple of weeks, and he'll probably give me the go-ahead then."

We rode quietly for a while. Jeff said, "Pete didn't think this was a good idea, us coming up here?"

"No."

Jeff's hands tightened on the steering wheel. "I want to look him in the face."

"I know. I'm mostly curious. And I want to ask him if he's serious about not contesting the will."

Jeff shot me a look of surprise. "You think he might?"

"Pete thought it was awfully coincidental that Barkley was getting paroled at exactly the same time his father's estate was finalized."

"Would he be successful? Might the will be overturned?"

"Kevin said he doubted it. There has to be evidence that the person who wrote the will wasn't in his right mind or was coerced to write it as he did. Gordon Smith didn't indicate that was the case."

"Good." Jeff squirmed in his seat a little. "I know I said I didn't want the money at first, but now that I have plans for it, I'd hate to not get it."

"What else are you going to do with it?"

"Pay the mortgage on the house, pay Dad back what we borrowed from him to buy it in the first place, and update the irrigation systems both at our place and Val's parents' farm. The rest we'll keep for the boys' education and emergencies and our own retirement." He glanced at me. "What will you do with the money?"

"We're going to look at property in New Mexico for a second home. Someplace to go when the Big One hits."

"Assuming you can get out of LA after the Big One hits."

"Yeah, well, there is that. Otherwise - we're going to remodel our bathrooms. We haven't talked about anything else."

"What's Kevin going to do?"

"I don't know. We haven't discussed it."

"What's going on with him and Abby?"

"Mm. I haven't said this to him, but I think her ex might be back in the picture."

"You think she's *cheating* on Kevin?"

"No, I don't think so. But she got squirrely like this once before, when we were all living together, four or five years ago. Turned out he'd been calling her, wanting to see her, asking for money."

Jeff frowned. "I thought she had more sense than that."

"Apparently not."

"Kevin's never had much luck with the ladies, has he?"

"No, and I'm not sure why."

Jeff looked at me as if it was obvious. "He's picked the wrong ones."

"Well, duh. The question is *why*."

"I don't know." Jeff frowned. "Kevin needs to be challenged. He picked a college major and a profession that are challenging, but he doesn't seem to make the correlation with his personal life."

"Maybe he feels that his job is such a challenge, at the end of the day he doesn't want to be challenged anymore."

Jeff shot me a skeptical look. "Do you really believe that?"

I laughed. "No."

"Don't get me wrong, Jennifer and Abby are both bright enough, but neither one of them is - um - intellectually substantive."

I grinned. "You're such an elitist, Dr. Brodie."

"Yeah, like you aren't, Dr. Brodie."

"You're right, though. Abby doesn't read at all. Her idea of intellectual stimulation is going to the movies. Jennifer's was - well, I don't know what Jennifer's was."

Jeff laughed. "Hiding sales receipts?"

I snorted. "Yeah, if that was an Olympic event, Jennifer would have racked up the gold."

"Do you think Kevin believes he's not smart enough for a really smart woman?"

I considered that. "No. I don't think he's got an inferiority complex in terms of intelligence. What I think is that he hasn't met a lot of women that he's been attracted to who are willing to put up with a cop's schedule or salary. And it's not like he comes across a lot of classy ladies in his work."

"Ha. No."

"I remember when he met Abby, he was really impressed with the fact that she was a master carpenter. That she was a woman successfully making her way in that man's world. He liked her toughness, which is something that Jennifer didn't have."

"That's true. Jennifer was a marshmallow."

"She was a kindergarten teacher. What do you expect?"

"He needs someone tough *and* intellectual. More like Val, for example."

I agreed. "But he's got to decide what to do about Abby first."

By the time we stopped for a late lunch at a Wendy's along the 5, the tension between us was easing - although I was still somewhat on my guard, hypersensitive to everything Jeff said.

It would take a bit longer for that to wear off.

Jeff nodded at my ring as we were sitting across the table from each other. "You ready to get married?"

"Um - in terms of wedding planning? Pretty much."

"I didn't mean that. I meant - ready in terms of 'as long as you both shall live.'"

"Yeah, I am. I think."

He laughed. "It's like having a kid. If you waited until you were one hundred percent sure you were ready for one, you might never have one."

I grinned. "Yeah, it's like that. But I'm ninety-nine percent sure. Pete's thoroughly vetted by now. And we've lived together for nearly three years in a fairly small space without killing each other."

Jeff chuckled. "The surest sign of true love." His expression sobered. "It does change things, though. Even if you've lived with someone first."

Jeff and Val had lived together their senior year of college. I said, "You know, I've heard people say that, but they never can explain how it changes."

"I'm not sure I can either." Jeff moved his straw in his cup, making the ice rattle. "It's another beginning, even though little about your day-to-day life might change. The knowledge that now you're truly in it for the long haul, that now it's going to take a hell of a lot more effort to break you apart - it's an attitude adjustment, I guess, more than anything. And also a feeling that now, you're really a team. Your marriage is a separate entity from either one of you individually." He looked up at me. "And the marriage requires as much care and feeding as each individual does. Every day. It's a lot of work."

"We're good communicators. I think we'll be okay. But thanks for the advice."

He smiled. "I wouldn't be much of a big brother if I didn't give you advice, would I?"

We drove into Folsom, checked into our room and took a few minutes to call home. When Pete answered, I heard familiar voices in the background. "Hey, where are you?"

"At Liz and Jon's. They invited Kevin and me over for dinner. Are you at your hotel?"

"Yep. We're gonna get Mexican food after a while. Where's Abby?"

"She stayed home. Said she had work to do."

"That's - um -"

"Yeah. We're not talking about that this evening."

"Okay. Is Liz cooking?"

"Yep."

"Is Jon drinking?"

"Some. He and Kev are off tomorrow."

"Okay. Have fun."

He laughed. "On it. I'll text you when I get home."

"Good. Love you."

"Love you, too."

When I hung up, Jeff was saying into his phone, "You can't have it both ways, Col. Either you share with Gabe or you don't use the telescope. Hogging it for yourself isn't an option." He listened patiently for a while. "I know, that's why Mom will supervise. He'll probably get tired of it after a bit, and then you'll have it to yourself for the rest of the night. No, I'm sorry, you don't get to claim schoolwork on a Saturday night." He rolled his eyes at me. "Okay. I think that's the right decision. Yes, it is fair. Fair doesn't mean always getting what *you* want." He laughed. "Yeah, wouldn't that be nice? Let me talk to Mom again."

When he hung up, I said, "You're a good dad."

"I try." He rubbed his eyes. "Colin's hormones are stirring, so he's more emotional, and Gabe's decided he's hot shit because he's going to middle school next year. *And* he's decided that it's fun to torment Colin."

"Like Kevin used to torment you."

"Exactly." He sighed. "I swear, a hundred times a day I find myself counting to ten and asking myself, 'What would Dad do?'"

"You can't go wrong there."

"No, I can't." He smiled at me. "Any kids in your future?"

"God, no. Only yours and Christine's." Pete's sister, mother to his teenage nieces.

"Good. 'Cause I don't know about Christine, but I'm gonna need all the help I can get."

Sunday, April 13

The next morning, we settled for the hotel's continental breakfast. Jeff's volubility of the previous day was gone; he seemed tense.

Walking into a prison felt claustrophobic, even though I knew I'd only be there a short while. We went through the extensive process of getting through the prison gates before we were ushered into a sunny room with a table and chairs. We didn't sit. Jeff was standing with his hands in his pockets, rocking up onto his toes and back down. A sign of nerves for him.

When the door opened, I turned. The man who was led through the door by the guard had clearly been handsome as a young man, and his face was still attractive, even with its prison pallor. Gavin Barkley didn't carry himself like a cocky rich boy, though. He was slightly stooped, thin, wearing glasses that gave him an academic air.

The guard closed the door and positioned himself in the corner, statue-like. Barkley sat at the table and looked up at us. "Thank you for coming. Won't you sit down?"

I sat across from him. Jeff stayed up, in the opposite corner from the guard. Barkley studied us. "Brodie. There were three of you."

I said, "Our middle brother thought this was a bad idea."

Jeff said, "He's a cop."

"Yes. And you're a veterinarian, and you -" He turned back to face me. "A librarian. My father's attorney has followed your lives."

I said, "That's creepy."

"I understand. But my father wanted to leave his estate to all of you. The survivors. So he needed to know where you were."

I said, "He left you nothing."

Barkley shrugged. "It wouldn't have done me any good in here. And when I'm released, I want to be able to make it on my own."

I said, "You're not going to contest the will?"

He gave me an even stare. "I told you I wouldn't. And I won't."

"What will you do when you get out?"

"I've earned a certificate in addictions counseling. I want to work with other released felons."

I said, "That's noble."

He gave me a weak smile. "When I wrote those letters, I doubted that any of you would respond. May I ask why you did?"

I said, "We wanted to put a face to the person who'd changed our lives so drastically."

He cocked his head, watching me. "You know, I actually thought during the first half of the trial that I'd get off. But then the prosecution started bringing you all in. First the kids of the other woman that died, then the lady in the back seat who'd been paralyzed, then you three." His gaze drifted to the wall. "You were adorable in your little matching outfits." His eyes shifted to Jeff. "You never stopped crying, the whole time you were there. Not out loud, just sniffling a little, big fat tears rolling down your cheeks. That's when I knew for sure that I was going to jail."

Jeff didn't make a sound.

I said, "And then your girlfriend."

"Katie." Gavin shook his head, staring at the table. "Most of the people in the courtroom were crying by the time her parents were done testifying. Hell, most of the people on the jury were crying."

"Did your father keep tabs on her too?"

"Yeah." Gavin didn't look up from the table. "She died twelve years after the accident, in a nursing home."

Jeff said, "Three murders."

Gavin raised his head, but he looked at me. "Yes." He swallowed. "I'm sure this means nothing to you, but for what it's worth, I'm sorry. If I could trade my life for your mother's, I would."

I shrugged. "But you can't."

"No." His gaze drifted to the wall again. "I can't."

I studied Gavin for a moment. He felt my gaze and looked back at me. "What?"

"Who's Jennelle Shifflett?"

Suddenly his expression animated. His eyes narrowed and he looked younger - and pissed. "I never met her."

"That's not what I asked."

Gavin pursed his lips - deciding what to say? "She's the other reason I want nothing to do with anything of my father's."

Aha. Must have been a mistress. "Gordon Smith said she was an old friend of the family."

He snorted in disgust. "So that's what they're calling it these days."

There wasn't much else to say. Jeff and I left shortly thereafter. Jeff was silent, but there were high points of red on his cheekbones and his fists were clenched.

He was angry. Again.

This was a side of Jeff I'd barely seen in adulthood. I thought it came from working with animals - patience with patients who couldn't speak to him. Val said the only time he ever got mad was when someone brought an abused animal to his practice.

But whatever was going on inside him now, Jeff was *mad*.

I saw road rage as a distinct possibility. I said, "Do you want me to drive?"

He didn't answer, just tossed me the keys.

Once we were away from Folsom and safely on the 80, I glanced at him. "Jeff?"

"What?"

"What's going on?"

"He shouldn't be alive."

"No, he shouldn't. In a just world, he would have been the only one to suffer. We don't live in a just world."

"No fucking shit."

That was a surprise. Jeff wasn't nearly as profane as Kevin or me. I said, "Is there more to it than that?"

"Why?"

"Because I've never seen you this pissed off."

"You have no idea how pissed off I am."

"Which just proves my point. Jeff, c'mon. What's going on?"

"Don't play psychologist with me."

"Oh, for God's sake. Stop it. I'm not playing psychologist. I'm just trying to find out, as your little brother, what's eating you so bad. But if you'd rather ride back to LA in silence, fine with me."

He didn't respond for a minute, then his taut expression collapsed a bit. "I'm sorry. I'm not mad at you. It's just so fucking *wrong*."

"It is *absolutely* fucking wrong."

He shook his head slowly, biting his lip, and it became clear. His tears at the trial, his fear of betraying our mom, his recognition of Drew Jemison, the green football… "You remember her, don't you?"

His eyes filled with tears. He tried to hold it back but failed. He sucked in a sobbing breath and started to cry.

I reached behind me with one hand to find the box of tissues that I knew was back there somewhere, came up with it and handed it to him. He accepted it and blew his nose. I said, "You've always said you didn't."

He nodded, tears still streaming. "Dad was so upset when I tried to talk about her. I couldn't stand it when he cried. So I pretended, as I got older, that I didn't remember."

"Oh, Jeff. Holding it in all this time…"

"I know." He blew his nose again and took a fresh tissue.

"Does Val know?"

"She does now."

"What do you remember?"

He sniffed. "Mostly impressions. But I remember her reading to me at bedtime, when you were too little and Kevin wouldn't hold still. My favorite book was Charlotte's Web. She read from it every night."

"How do you remember that?"

"I don't know. It's the only thing I do remember. Other than that, it's not much. Just flashes of her being in the kitchen. Ironing Dad's uniforms. That's about it."

"Uncle Doug asked me last year whether you remembered her. I asked him why he thought you did, and he said you'd asked where she was every day for about a year. He figured that you finally realized she wasn't coming back."

"I guess that's partly true. But I also knew that when I asked about her, it made Daddy cry. I didn't want to make him cry."

I reached over and squeezed his arm. "Kevin said once that he wished he remembered her, and I said I thought it might be worse if we did. It's worse, isn't it?"

He nodded and blew his nose again.

"Will you tell Dad?"

He nodded.

Thursday, April 16

The following few days were so busy that I didn't have time to think about Gavin Barkley, being rich, getting married or anything except work. On Thursday, I was eating lunch at my desk, grading history papers, when my dad texted me. *Call when you can.*

I called. "Hey, Dad, what's up?"

He said, "Gavin Barkley was released from prison yesterday."

"Ah, right. What about it?"

"He called me."

"*What??* When?"

"This morning. I'd taken Colin to the library. When I got back, Barkley had left a message on the land line answering machine."

"What did he say?"

My dad's tone expressed his disbelief. "He said he was sorry for what he'd done and asked for forgiveness."

"Did he want you to call him *back?*"

"No. He didn't leave a number. He said he just wanted me to know."

"Holy *shit.*"

"I know. I wanted to give you a heads-up in case he's going down the list."

"He apologized to Jeff and me when we saw him. I doubt he'll call us. But you might want to warn the Marcuses."

"Damn, you're right. Do you still have the number?"

"They're in your phone book. If he called you this morning, he may have already called them."

"Yeah." Dad's voice was grim. "I'll let you know."

I went to the reference desk worrying about my dad and Belinda Marcus. What was Gavin thinking? He'd had thirty-four years to write letters of apology. He'd written letters to the children; why was he calling the adults?

Liz had come straight from a research instruction session; she dropped into her seat and peeled open a granola bar. "God, I'm starving." She saw my expression and frowned. "What's wrong?"

I told her about Gavin's call. She said, "Jeez. Does he *want* to upset them?"

"I doubt it. I'm sure he sees it as part of his clean slate. But he didn't stop to think about how they'd react."

When Clinton approached the desk I said, "Hi, Clinton, do you have a minute?"

He looked surprised; we hadn't had an actual conversation in about a month. "Of course." He sat across from me, patiently expectant.

I explained, as briefly as I could, who Gavin was and about the phone call. I didn't tell him about the inheritance - not that I didn't trust Clinton, because I did, but I'd do it in a more private place. "Why would he wait until now to apologize?"

Clinton steepled his fingers, thinking. "I believe that you are correct. He considers the apologies to be the springboard for his new life. I doubt that he considered the effect it might have on your father and friends. He may also be going down a checklist of sorts, such as the twelve steps that addiction counselors recommend."

Liz said, "Why wait until he got out? He hasn't been drinking for thirty-four years. Looks like he would have wanted to complete the steps a long time ago."

"I agree, the logic is somewhat faulty." He smiled gently. "I must be on my way, but I will leave you with a calming word." He stood. "The word of the day is *xyst*." He bowed and walked away.

Liz looked it up. "Oh, nice. A garden walk planted with trees."

I closed my eyes briefly, imagining. Then I looked it up on Google Images and started scrolling through the beautiful pictures.

That evening, Dad called back. "By the time I talked to Belinda, Barkley had already called her. She was in a panic."

"No doubt. What did he say to her?"

"That he was sorry for all the pain he'd caused, that he was rebuilding his life, that he hoped she could find it in her heart to forgive him someday. She told him, 'Don't ever contact me again,' and he said he wouldn't and he didn't mean to upset her. That was it."

"Clinton suggested that he might be in some twelve-step program, marking items off a checklist."

"That might explain it."

I grumbled. "That's always pissed me off. People going through their twelve steps, thinking once they finish they can go on their merry way. It's always seemed like it's more about them than the people they hurt."

Dad said, "I've known a lot of people who've turned their lives around through those programs. But I've seen what you're talking about, too. Usually those folks were narcissistic before, and the twelve steps don't necessarily change that."

"I'd guess that Gavin Barkley was pretty damn narcissistic."

Dad laughed drily. "I'd guess that's right."

Friday, April 17

On Friday, I got a call from Michelle Richardson, my high school classmate who was now Gordon Smith's legal assistant. "Jamie, do you have a secure fax number?"

"Uh - yeah." The fax machine in Special Collections in the basement of our building was as secure as they came.

"Good. I'm going to send you the official notification of the settlement of Randall Barkley's estate."

"Ah." I gave her the number. "Thanks, Michelle."

"You're welcome." She laughed. "Mel's gonna be glad she's your attorney."

"Um - okay?"

"I'm sending it as we speak. You might want to go to the machine now."

"On my way."

I trotted down to the basement and swiped my BruinCard to get access to Special Collections. Demetrius Garmon, one of our Special Collections librarians, was leaning in the doorway of director Conrad Huffstetler's office. Demetrius grinned at me. "Hey, what brings you to the tombs?"

"I'm getting a fax from an attorney's office, and I routed it here. Hope that's okay."

Conrad said, "Absolutely. Go on back."

I went down the hall to the fax/copier/mail room, where I had to punch in a combination. Special Collections dealt with rare and expensive items, and security was a big deal. When I opened the door, the fax machine was humming. I pulled the paper out as it came through, flipped it over and stared at it.

$37,823,955.47.

The letter, signed by Gordon Smith, said that the money would be available in approximately three weeks. His office would need our bank account numbers before the transfer took place; they would give us the precise date as soon as possible.

I took a deep breath and blew it out. Until now, the money had been an abstraction. Six hundred and eighty million dollars, floating around out there somewhere. Now here it was, down to the last penny, in black ink.

Holy shit.

What was I going to do with all this? What were any of us going to do?

Saturday, April 18

We'd scheduled a hike for Saturday morning - Kevin, Abby, Jon, Liz, Pete and me. We'd also invited Justin Como, one of our fellow librarians at YRL, and Lance Scudieri, one of Pete's former students, now a UCLA student and full-time library circulation tech. Justin and Lance had been seeing each other for a few months - a relationship engineered by Liz, but it seemed to be flourishing. Justin had been closeted when he'd arrived at UCLA, and Lance had been good for him, bringing him out and easing him into LA gay society gradually.

I was tying my boots when my phone buzzed with two texts - one from Kevin, one from Liz. Kevin's said, *Jon and I have a body up Benedict Canyon. Abby's bugging out too - SAYS she has to work. Sorry. Catch up with you later*. Liz's said, *Jon and Kevin have a body. I'll see you there.*

I texted back *okay* to both and stood, thinking, my gaze directed at my phone but not seeing it. Pete had been loading his backpack; now he noticed me staring at my phone. "What?"

"Oh. Kevin and Jon have a body, and Abby supposedly has to work."

"Where's the DB?"

I huffed a laugh. "Benedict Canyon, Officer Ferguson."

He grinned. "Sorry. Abby has to work on a Saturday?"

"That's what she says. I don't believe her."

"I don't remember her ever working on Saturday before." Before Kevin and Abby started having problems.

"She didn't. She's in the union, so when they work weekends they get mega-overtime. The studios try to avoid paying that."

Pete's brow furrowed. "Could Abby be cheating on Kevin?"

"Jeff wondered about that too, but I don't think so. I think she has something else going on that she doesn't want Kev to know about."

"Hm." Pete wasn't convinced.

Neither was I.

When we got to the parking lot at Topanga Canyon, Lance and Justin were waiting for us. We chatted with them, waiting for Liz. When she pulled in five minutes later, we saw that she'd brought an extra.

Kristen Beach was another YRL librarian, a friend of Liz's and mine for several years. She was in her late thirties but looked younger. At work she always dressed to play with the sexy librarian stereotype - dark hair in a bun, red lipstick, black-framed glasses, white blouse, black pencil skirt and stilettos. Away from the library, though, she was a gym rat, always willing to participate in anything involving exercise. She was financially comfortable thanks to an extremely favorable divorce settlement a few years ago which left her with a home in Bel Air and a couple of million dollars.

Kristen was one of the funniest people I knew and hands down the most profane woman I'd ever met. She'd teamed up with Mel to get Justin released after he was wrongly arrested in the Stacks Strangler case a year and a half ago. She was formidable, and one of my favorite people.

Kristen hopped out of the car, her hair in a ponytail this morning. She was wearing a t-shirt, cargo shorts and hiking boots, but still looked hot - even I could appreciate that. She grinned at us. "Hey, guys. Couldn't let Liz have all the fun today."

We greeted Kristen and headed up the trail. Liz paired up with Pete, and they were soon in deep discussion. Justin and Lance were ahead; I dropped back with Kristen. "What's going on with Lawrence?" Kristen's on-again, off-again boyfriend.

She waved her hand in dismissal. "Lawrence is an asshole. His wife's back from her sabbatical or whatever it was in Santa Fe, and he let her move right back in."

"Did she become a shaman?"

"Who the hell knows? Lawrence said that it didn't mean we couldn't still see each other. I said, 'The fuck it doesn't' and told him to get out."

"He was married before, he's married now - what's the difference?"

She gave me a light smack on the arm. "For a gay guy, you're a real Puritan sometimes. He was legally *separated* before. Now he's openly, sleeping-in-the-same-bed married. I don't share."

"Good for you. So you're single now?"

"Yes. And staying that way, thank you very much."

"Nah. You'll find someone else."

"Ha. You just say that because you're so happy. You want everyone to have what you and Pete do."

I grinned, looking at Pete's back. "Would that be such a bad thing?"

Kristen just laughed.

We hiked all morning, enjoying ourselves immensely. When we got back to the parking lot, Liz said, "Want to grab some lunch somewhere?"

Lance said, "Oh, that sounds good, but we're going to look at apartments this afternoon."

Liz and I made pleased sounds. I said, "That's great, guys."

"Yeah." Justin blushed. "We figured it was time."

Lance got in the car and waved. "See you at work."

Pete said, "Well, I'm up for lunch. Jamie?"

"Sure. Kristen, you coming?"

"Of course."

We agreed to meet at 800 Degrees in Westwood for pizza and headed back to town. On the way, I got a text from Kevin. *Where are you?*

On our way to eat. You done?

For now. Liz with you?

Yeah, and Kristen from work. Meet us at 800 Degrees?

See you there.

Jon pulled into a parking space not long after we did. Both he and Kevin were rumpled and unhappy, but they both brightened on scenting pizza.

Kevin gave Kristen a curious look. I said, "Have you two met?"

Both said at the same time, "I don't think so."

We laughed. I said, "Kristen Beach, Kevin Brodie. Hey, you've got the same initials."

Kristen grinned. "Well, then, we have to be friends. Kevin, it's good to meet you."

Kevin smiled. "My pleasure."

After we'd ordered and gotten seated, Jon said, "How was your hike?"

Liz said, "It was great. How was your body?"

Jon scrunched up his face. "She was dead."

Kevin said, "Um - maybe Kristen doesn't want to hear this."

Kristen said, "Oh, I don't mind. I find forensics fascinating."

Jon shot her a grin. "She was a Jane Doe, mid-thirties. Really attractive girl, shot in the chest around midnight last night and dumped in the canyon. She was moved after she was killed. We haven't found the primary scene yet."

Pete said, "No ID?"

"Nope. She didn't have a purse, keys, anything."

"Robbery?"

"Maybe." But Jon didn't look convinced.

Kevin said, "I don't think she saw it coming. There were no wounds on her hands, like she'd thrown them up in front of her to protect herself. If she'd been robbed first, she should have had defensive wounds."

I said, "Maybe it happened too fast."

"Or maybe it was a murder staged to look like a robbery."

Pete asked, "Did you find the weapon?"

Jon said, "No. The bullet's in her, so that's in our favor. I'd guess a .38, but I could be wrong."

Kristen said, "How will you identify her?"

Kevin seemed surprised - but pleased - that she was expressing an interest. "The crime scene techs took her fingerprints, so we'll see if she's in the system. My bet is that she's not, but you never know. This afternoon, we'll go back to the station and search the missing persons database, see if she turns up. We'll get her autopsy pushed to the front of the line, too, to see if there's anything there that can identify her."

Kristen said, "It must be frustrating."

"Sometimes." Kevin gave Kristen a sideways smile. "We'll find out who she is, though. Then we'll find her killer."

I said, "Kevin's got the best homicide solve rate in LAPD."

Kristen grinned. "Doesn't surprise me a bit."

After lunch, we parted ways - Kevin and Jon heading for the police station, Liz and Kristen going to Kristen's house, Pete and I going home. When we were underway, I said, "What were you and Liz discussing so intently on the trail?"

"Oh." Pete scowled. "Liz found out what's up with Abby. Or at least part of it."

"What? And how? I thought Abby had decided she didn't like Liz."

"Apparently it's mostly Jon she doesn't like. And Liz and Jon together make her uncomfortable."

"Why, for God's sake?"

"Because they 'project an air of privilege.' Abby feels like they're looking down at her."

"*What?* That could not be *further* from the truth."

"I know that, but Abby's got this in her head somehow."

"Huh." I frowned out the window. "This is Andie's doing."

Pete shook his head. "Anyway, one evening a couple of weeks ago, Kevin and Jon had to work, and Liz called Abby to see if she wanted to go out. Abs was reluctant, but agreed, and after a couple of drinks she told Liz something and made her promise not to tell Jon, Kevin or you." He snorted a laugh. "She forgot about me."

"What is it?"

"Her ex has been calling her."

"Shit. I was afraid of this." Abby's ex, Sean Nichols, had been a lighting guy at the studios. He'd developed serious drug problems; Abby had divorced him after his third stint in rehab failed. "Why?"

"He wants her help getting his job back. He's asked her for money. He says he still loves her."

"She's not *seeing* him, is she?"

"Not like that. She's not cheating on Kevin. She's met with him several times and has given him some money."

"Her own money, or hers and Kevin's?"

"Both."

"Oh *no*." Jennifer had lied to Kevin about money - in her case, how much she was spending. "If Kev finds out Abby's been giving Sean their money, he'll shit bricks."

"I know."

We both brooded on that a moment. I said, "So why is Abs picking these fights? Would she rather break up with Kevin than tell him what she's doing?"

"Maybe." Pete looked grim. "Kevin won't break up with her. She'll have to do it."

"He might if he finds out about this. Are you going to tell him?"

"Abby swore Liz to secrecy, not me. I think he has a right to know. What do you think?"

"I think it would cause a lot of damage between him and us if he ever found out that we knew and didn't tell him."

He nodded. "I think you're right."

That evening, Pete and I accepted a dinner invitation from our friends Aaron Quinn and Paul Thayer. Aaron and Paul had gotten married on New Year's Eve in the backyard of their house in Pasadena. We'd had difficulty deciding what to get them as a gift; they'd lived together for several years and had everything. We'd decided on a piece of art - sort of.

Aaron and Paul's home was a gallery of phallic art. Paintings and sculptures - and in their bedroom, photographs - of the erect penis were everywhere. The one thing they didn't have was a custom-made wood carving. I'd commissioned Abby to put on her sculpting hat and create one for me, and she'd outdone herself, using oak. Aaron and Paul had been delighted with it.

When Paul let us in, we handed him the bottle of wine we'd brought and followed him back to the kitchen. When we passed the dining room, Paul paused, reached around the door frame and flipped on the light. "Voila."

Abby's carving was serving as the centerpiece for the dining room table. I could only laugh.

Aaron, like Pete, was a fabulous cook. We gathered around the breakfast bar to watch him in action. Paul said, "How is your brother's lovely girlfriend who created that masterpiece for us?"

I accepted a glass of wine. "Still lovely, but maybe not my brother's girlfriend for long."

Aaron said, "Uh oh. Trouble in paradise?"

I wouldn't have ever called it paradise, but... "Yeah. There are major issues."

Paul said, "They're not married, are they?"

"No. Fortunately."

"Well then. Your brother can just walk away."

"I hope so."

Aaron waved a spatula at us. "No depressing talk. How are you guys coming with the wedding planning?"

Pete and I looked at each other and laughed. "There's not much to plan."

Aaron and Paul's wedding had been small but lavish. They'd worn white tuxes and rented a champagne fountain. Pete said, "We're gonna climb a mountain, say our vows, climb back down the mountain and go to Neil and Mark's house to drink a few beers."

Paul rolled his eyes. "You guys are so *butch*."

I said, "You two are coming, right? July 3rd." We'd sent out save-the-date e-cards back in February.

Aaron smiled. "We wouldn't miss it."

Dinner was delicious, and we stayed late afterward, Aaron, Paul and I drinking wine and telling stories about the weddings we'd been to in our lives. Pete, as our designated driver, had only drunk one glass of wine before dinner and stuck to water for the rest of the evening.

We left shortly after ten. I was pleasantly buzzed, still chuckling to myself about some of the stories of wedding excess that Paul had told. Pete glanced at me and grinned. "You're happy."

"I'm full of good food and wine, I'm engaged to the most wonderful guy on the planet and I've got $38 million coming my way. Who wouldn't be happy?"

Pete laughed. "When you put it like that…"

I poked him gently in the ribs. "We are butch, aren't we? We're getting married like lumberjacks."

"Are you bringing an axe?"

That got me giggling. "Maybe we could have them at the reception. Instead of a goodie bag for the guests, everyone gets an axe."

Pete started singing. "I'm a lumberjack, and I'm okay…"

We laughed all the way back to Santa Monica.

Part 2

"If you prick us, do we not bleed? … if you poison us, do we not die? and if you wrong us, shall we not revenge?" - William Shakespeare, The Merchant of Venice, Act III, Scene I

Sunday, April 19

On Sunday, we had chores to catch up on. Right after breakfast, I went outside to power-wash the front walk. Pete was doing the monthly cleaning of the fridge. I hadn't been working very long when our gate opened and a man and a woman approached.

Cops. I knew the man - Max O'Brien, LAPD homicide detective from Pacific Division, formerly Jon Eckhoff's partner. I didn't know the woman, but I figured she must be Max's new partner.

I turned off the washer. "Hey, Max. What's up?"

"Hi, Jamie. I'm afraid we're here on official business. This is my partner, Susan Portman."

Susan Portman was a blocky woman in chinos, a polo shirt and a windbreaker, with short, spiked dark hair. She held out her hand. "Dr. Brodie."

"Detective. Come on inside."

We went in; Susan and Max took the sofa. I called up to the kitchen. "Pete, the police are here."

"Oh?" He trotted downstairs. "Hi, Max."

"Hi. This is my new partner, Susan Portman."

Pete nodded to Susan. "What's up?"

Susan was frowning slightly. "Would it be possible to speak to the two of you separately?"

What the hell? Pete said, "Uh - sure. I'll go finish the front walk." He went outside, and I heard the power washer start up.

I sat down on the loveseat. "How can I help you?"

Susan said, "Before we begin, let me say that Detective O'Brien has informed me of his previous interactions with you. I don't see a conflict of interest."

"Good." I gave Max a small nod. "What's going on?"

Max said, "May I record this conversation?"

"You may."

He switched on the recorder on his phone. Susan took out a notepad - old school. "First, Dr. Brodie, can you tell us where you were last night?"

"Um - we left here about 5:00 and drove up to Pasadena to have dinner with friends. We were there until about 10:15. Then we came home, watched some TV and went to bed."

"Can you give me the name and address of your friends?"

"Aaron Quinn and Paul Thayer." I gave her the address.

"Who drove home?"

"Pete did. I'd had a couple of glasses of wine."

"So you arrived home at what time?"

"Um - oh, I forgot, we stopped at Vons to get a few things. We got home around 11:30. Do you want to see the receipt?"

"If you have it, that would be helpful."

"Okay, it's upstairs." I started to stand up.

Susan motioned me back down. "We'll take a look at it when we're finished."

I sat. "Yes, ma'am."

"Do you remember what you watched on TV?"

I winced. "Yes, ma'am. Ancient Aliens."

She cocked an eyebrow at me. "*Really.*"

I gave her a sheepish smile. "It's kind of a guilty pleasure."

"All right. You didn't leave the house once you got home?"

"No, ma'am."

"And I assume that Dr. Ferguson will confirm all of this?"

"He will." I looked back and forth between Max and Susan. "May I ask whose body you've found?"

Susan cocked an eyebrow. "Detective O'Brien tells me you're pretty comfortable with homicide investigations."

I grimaced. "I wish I wasn't."

It seemed that Susan relaxed a bit. "The body of Gavin Barkley was found along the Venice boardwalk at approximately 5:00 this morning."

My jaw dropped. I closed my mouth, then opened it again and blew out a breath. "Holy *shit*. He was *murdered?*"

"When did you last see Barkley?"

"I've only seen him once in my life - I mean, once in my adult life, and that was one week ago today at Folsom Prison."

"Why did you go see him?"

I said bleakly, "He was in jail for killing my mom and one of her friends. We'd only recently learned his name and we just - we wanted to see his face."

"When you say we, who do you mean?"

I swallowed. "My brother Jeff and me."

"Your brother Kevin didn't go with you?"

"No. He thought it was a bad idea."

Susan looked like she thought it was a bad idea too. "You said you'd only seen him once as an adult. What do you mean by that?"

"I was a year old when Barkley went to trial. My dad took my brothers and me to the courtroom one day at the request of the prosecutor."

"All right." Susan leaned back against the sofa. "Why don't you go get that receipt for us now?"

I raced upstairs and snatched the receipt from my desk, mentally thanking the gods that I was an organized person. When I handed it to Susan, she wrote down the details from it then handed it back to me. "Do you happen to know where your brother Jeff was yesterday?"

I stared at her for a second, trying to remember whether anyone had told me Jeff and Val's plans for the weekend. "No, ma'am."

"Do you own a gun?"

Oh, shit. "No, ma'am. But Pete has two here at the house."

"What are they?"

"A Glock 9mm and a .20-gauge shotgun."

"Does your brother Jeff own a gun?"

"No, ma'am."

Susan studied me for a minute then seemed to come to a decision. "Barkley's death was staged to look like a suicide. He was killed with a .38. Do you know anyone that owns one of those?"

Thank God. "No, ma'am. Um - are you sure it wasn't a suicide?"

Max said, "He was shot in the right side of the head. Barkley was left-handed."

I said, "Pfft. *That* was dumb."

Susan looked faintly amused. "Have you ever met any of the children of the other accident victims?"

"Yes, ma'am, two of them. Josh Marcus and Drew Jemison."

"Where and when did you meet them?"

"At the office of Barkley's father's attorney, two weeks ago."

"Have you had any other contact with them?"

"No, ma'am." I remembered my conversation with my dad earlier in the week. "Barkley called my dad and Belinda Marcus."

"Yes, Kevin told us. Did that make your father angry?"

"He wasn't angry. He was more - dismayed. Barkley left a message, so Dad didn't actually have to speak to him. He wanted to warn us in case Barkley was calling everyone. But Barkley had already apologized to us when we saw him in prison. We didn't hear from him."

"Do you know if he called anyone else?"

"I don't know."

Susan glanced at Max, who said, "Do you happen to know if Gavin Barkley was going to contest his father's will?"

"I asked him that at the prison. He said he wasn't."

Susan asked, "How much are you getting?"

"About thirty-eight million each."

Max whistled. Susan said, "That's a nice piece of change."

"That's the understatement of the year. Ma'am."

Susan grinned, and I liked her better. Max said, "If he *was* thinking about challenging the will, and he mentioned it to someone…"

I said, "That's a pretty good motive."

Susan stood up and slapped her notebook closed. "And *that's* the understatement of the year."

Susan and Max stopped on the sidewalk to talk to Pete for a few minutes then left. Pete came inside just as my phone rang.

It was Kevin. I said, "Hey. Susan Portman and Max O'Brien just left."

"Ah, good. They woke me up at 4:30 this morning."

"They figured out our connection with Barkley pretty fast."

"Well, yeah, they got the visitor logs from the prison. Max recognized your name, and they decided to call me first."

"Do you know anyone that owns a .38?"

"No one that would be involved in this. I don't even think Dad has one."

Dad, being a former gunnery sergeant and weapons instructor, had several firearms, but I knew none of them were .38s. "No, he doesn't. Did you have a good alibi?"

"Yeah. Abby and I were at Amy's house until about 11:30, then we put gas in the truck on the way home, so we had a receipt. They figure Barkley was killed between ten and midnight."

"Ah, they didn't tell me that."

Kevin sighed. "Listen, it would be best if you didn't talk to Jeff or Dad until the police have. It'll help keep the waters less muddied."

After lunch, Pete got busy in the kitchen doing prep work for our meals for the coming week. I dusted and vacuumed the house then decided to get some fresh air. I went out front and examined our herb beds, spotted a few weeds, and squatted down to pull them. I was still rooting around in the dirt when a voice said, "Hello?"

I looked up to see a woman standing there. She looked close to my dad's age. She was petite, with short but stylish silver-blond hair, dressed in a long skirt, t-shirt and vest, wearing ballet flats, carrying a large bag. I scrambled to my feet. "Can I help you?"

Her expression shifted from curiosity to recognition. "Jamie."

"Do I know you?"

She smiled tightly and held out her hand. "I'm Marie Crabtree."

"*Oh.*" I brushed the dirt off and shook her hand - which was cold. "I'm - uh - hi."

Her smile didn't waver. "I'm sorry to come unannounced. I was in Oceanside and stopped to see Belinda, and she mentioned that you'd been to see her."

"Yes, ma'am. Um - would you like to come in?"

"If I'm not interrupting. I don't want to disrupt your plans."

I gestured to the plants. "I've just finished. Come on in."

I led Marie into the living room and said, "Pete? We have company."

He stuck his head around the cabinets to look down into the living room. "Oh?" He picked up a dish towel and came downstairs, drying his hands.

I said, "Mrs. Crabtree, this is my fiancé, Pete Ferguson. Pete, this is Marie Crabtree. One of my mom's friends."

"Oh. *Oh.*" Pete held out his hand. "Glad to meet you, Mrs. Crabtree."

"You too, Pete. And please call me Marie. I told Jamie, I don't want to interrupt your day."

Pete gestured to the kitchen. "I'm in the middle of chopping some vegetables."

"Don't let me keep you from your chopping."

I said, "Can I get you anything to drink? Iced tea?"

"Yes, thank you."

I followed Pete upstairs and got Marie a glass of tea. "Please, sit down."

She looked around. "This is lovely. Have you lived here long?"

I said, "I've been here nearly three years. Pete lived here before that. It belonged to his great-uncle."

"Ah." Marie smiled again, but it didn't reach her eyes. "I thought perhaps you'd already been out spending some of that money."

I smiled back, thinking, *Even if you were my mom's friend, that's none of your business.* "No, ma'am."

"Belinda tells me that you're a librarian at UCLA."

"Yes, ma'am."

"That must be so *interesting*." She sipped her tea, but her eyes never left me.

"Most days, yes." I wished Pete would come downstairs. There was something off about Marie Crabtree, but I couldn't identify it.

She reached over and laid her hand on my arm. Her hand was clammy. "And how is your dad?"

I had the growing feeling that I shouldn't tell this lady anything. "He's fine."

I heard the refrigerator door open and close, and Pete came downstairs. "There we go." He sat beside me - between me and the loveseat where Marie had perched - and beamed at her. "Now we can visit properly."

I knew Pete hadn't had time to finish what he was doing. He must have heard something in Marie's voice or mine. And under normal circumstances he would have sat on my other side. He wanted to get close to Marie which, I suspected, was a ploy to rattle her.

She did move away from him a little under pretense of rearranging her skirt. "Indeed. I was telling Jamie, you have a beautiful home."

"Thank you." Pete was completely relaxed, smiling at Marie. The good cop. I'd seen him do this before. "Where do *you* live, Mrs. Crabtree?"

She fluttered a hand, suddenly coy. "Oh, you must call me Marie. We live in the Buckhead section of Atlanta."

Heh. Instantly proclaiming her social status, although Pete might not know about Buckhead. I said, "Ah, that's a gorgeous part of the city."

"It is. I love Atlanta. It's so - *vibrant*." She took another sip of tea. "Pete, what do you do?"

"I'm a criminal psychologist."

Marie's smile never wavered, but I saw a flash of something unsettled in her eyes. "That must be fascinating."

"Oh, it is."

She cleared her throat. "Do you work for the police department?"

"I was with LAPD for ten years. Now I teach and do research."

I said, "Do you remember my middle brother, Kevin?"

Marie turned her gaze to me, relaxing a bit. She must have thought we were changing the subject. "Yes, of course. How is he?"

"He's fine. He's a homicide detective with LAPD. He and Pete were partners for a while."

"My goodness." Her tinkling laugh sounded forced. "I'm surrounded by law enforcement."

Pete grinned at her. "You couldn't be safer."

Marie carefully set her glass on the coaster. "So you must be thrilled by the news of your inheritance. I know my daughter was."

Interesting that she didn't mention her son. I said, "Yes, ma'am. We were astounded."

"I'm sure you have big plans for the money."

What was she trying to find out? I said, "We're working on a wish list. How about your daughter?"

Her smile faded and her expression became tense. "As you say. She's building a wish list. She has student loans to pay off."

Pete said, "Wise decision."

"Yes." Marie took another sip of tea then stood. "Well, I've taken up enough of your time." She reached out and squeezed my hand. "Jamie, it's wonderful to see you doing so well. Please give my best to your dad."

"Thank you, ma'am. I will."

We walked her out to the sidewalk where she'd parked a rental car and watched her drive away. I said, "That was bizarre."

"Mm hm." Pete's expression was thoughtful. "She had an agenda, but I'm not sure what it was."

"I got the impression that she changed course when she found out who you were."

"Right. And that was smart, telling her about Kevin."

I shrugged. "If she's looking for someone to mess with, I wanted to make sure she knew she was barking up the wrong tree."

Pete scratched his chin and turned back toward the front door. "She didn't mention Gavin Barkley."

"She may not know he's dead." Then a thought struck me. "Or she may know perfectly well that he's dead."

Pete shot me a glance. "Because she killed him?"

"I bet Gavin called her, like he called Dad and Belinda. She was probably as rattled as Belinda was. What if she decided to come out here and do something about it?"

"Maybe." Pete locked the door behind us. "She's nervous about *something*."

Pete and I had settled onto the sofa for the evening, each with a book, when my phone rang. It was Val, and she was crying. That scared me. I'd never heard Val cry. I said, "What's wrong?"

"Jeff doesn't have an alibi for last night."

"What? Where was he?"

"He got called out yesterday about 6:30 for an emergency delivery of a colt, and said that I shouldn't hold dinner. He called about 9:30 and said the delivery had been really stressful, and he was going to the pier to unwind. He does that, sometimes."

I said, "He always has. When we were teenagers he'd go out there sometimes, just to look at the water."

"Right. He's done it before, so I didn't think anything about it. I texted him at about 10:30 and said I was going to bed, and he said okay. But he didn't come home until around 1:30. I thought he might have been at your dad's, but he said he'd gone to the beach and had lost track of time. I didn't think anything about it until the cops got here this afternoon."

"They came to see you?"

"Yeah. I guess they interviewed us, and your dad, and Mr. and Mrs. Marcus. Fortunately your dad spent the night with Barb, so he has an alibi." Val sucked in a shuddering breath. "I'm scared, Jamie. I know Jeff couldn't kill anyone, but..." Her voice trailed off.

I said, "You're right. He wouldn't kill anyone. There are tests they can do on his clothes and all, aren't there? For gunshot residue? There won't be any evidence."

"That's what Kevin said."

"See? Have you ever known Kevin and me to both be wrong about something?"

That made her laugh. "Plenty of times, Junior."

"Yeah, yeah. But not this time. Listen, I know one of these cops. Max O'Brien. He did his detective training with Kevin and Tim Garcia. He's good, and I was impressed with his partner. They'll clear Jeff. I know it's easy to say, but try not to worry."

She sighed. "I know. I'm trying. Talking to you helps."

"Good. Where is Jeff now?"

"He took the boys with him to go check on that new colt." I heard some scrabbling noise in the background, and Val yelled, "Ralphie! Get out of there!"

I laughed. "Go corral your dog, lady."

"Okay. Thanks, Jamie. Love you."

"Love you too." I ended the call and went to the kitchen. "Jeff doesn't have an alibi."

Pete's eyes widened. "Shit. Where was he?"

I explained. Pete shook his head. "At least he has a history of doing that. It doesn't look as bad as it might otherwise."

"Yeah." I scrubbed my hands through my hair. "This whole thing is turning into a nightmare."

The next morning, Kevin called. "Want to have lunch? I'll come to campus."

"Sure. Is Jon coming?"

"No, he's gone back to the neighborhood where we found our Jane Doe. Someone's remembered seeing a strange car. Probably nothing, so we didn't both have to go."

"And it keeps Jon busy."

Kevin laughed. "Yeah. You want tacos?"

A food truck that parked near the West LA Division station made the best tacos in this part of the city. "Sounds good." It occurred to me that I needed to tell Kevin about Abby and her ex. "Come to my office. I can officially work through lunch."

"Okay. See you at noon."

Kevin arrived promptly at noon with a big bag from the taco truck near the station. We divided them up on my desk, and Kevin pulled a chair up close to the desk. I said, "Why don't you shut the door? That way this deliciousness won't draw onlookers."

"Good idea." He closed the door and sat down.

I said, "What else is going on with your Jane Doe?"

"Mm." Kevin swallowed a bite of taco. "We got her autopsy done this morning. It didn't help."

"Were her fingerprints in the system?"

"No, and she doesn't fit the description of any of LAPD's missing persons. We were able to confirm that the bullet was a .38, and one of the coroner's investigators said that her clothing labels weren't from local stores."

"Can you track them down?"

"We're gonna try."

"Suppose she was a tourist?"

"I guess she could have been."

We ate quietly for a minute. I was trying to decide how to broach the subject of Abby when Kevin said, "I heard from Max this morning. He said that since Jeff was a suspect in Gavin Barkley's murder, they were going to keep me updated on their progress as a courtesy."

"Oh, good. Val called me crying last night."

"Yeah, me too. Anyway, they established a few more alibis. Tony Jemison and his daughter were at her house in Oregon, at a birthday party for one of the daughter's kids, with several guests."

"A late-night birthday party for a kid?"

"It was a sleepover with a bunch of eight-year-old boys. Tony was there to help with crowd control."

"Ah. What about the others?"

"Karen Marcus was on a Girl Scout camping trip. Josh was at Brian and Belinda's. Drew says he was home by himself but made several phone calls. The only Crabtree they talked to was the son, in Boston; he's an RN and was on shift at the hospital. They couldn't get hold of Alexandra Crabtree, and by then it was too late to call the parents."

I said, "Marie Crabtree was here."

"*What?*"

I told Kevin about her visit. "I need to call Max."

"Definitely."

"I'll do it this afternoon." Lunch was almost over; I had to tell Kevin about Abby. I took a deep breath and plunged in. "Listen, there's something else I have to tell you."

"About the case?"

"No. About Abby."

Kevin's expression became wary. "This is bad, right?"

I told him what Liz had told Pete. Kevin listened quietly, his scowl growing deeper. When I told him about the money, he pushed back from the desk and jumped to his feet. "God damn it." He paced for a few seconds then turned. "God *damn* it. She *knows* how I feel about Sean. *And* how I feel about using our money without discussing it."

"I know, Kev. I'm sorry."

He put his hands on his hips, shaking his head. "That's it, then."

"Are you going to tell her you know?"

"No. When are we getting this money? Two weeks?"

"About that, yeah."

"Then she's got two weeks to come clean. If she hasn't confessed by then, we're done. I'm not letting her give a penny of this inheritance to that scumbag."

"What are you going to do?"

"I don't know. I have to think about this."

"Okay. If you want to talk, you know where we are."

He looked at me, and his face softened a bit. "Thanks, short stuff."

"You know I'm always looking out for you."

"Yeah. I know." He wadded up the debris from our meal and hurled it into my trash can so hard that it nearly tipped over before settling back on its base. "I have to go track down those clothing labels."

"Okay. Don't Taze anybody."

He gave me a sharp look. "No promises."

After our reference shift, I went back to my office and called Max. When he answered, I said, "Hey, Max, I have some information for you."

"Pertaining to Gavin Barkley?"

"Yep." I told him about Marie's visit.

Max snorted a derisive laugh. "Well, how about that? We called the Crabtrees this morning, and all she admitted to was visiting Belinda in San Diego. That's what her husband thought she was doing, too."

"Nope. She left something out."

"I'll say. Okay, thanks, Jamie. We'll have to call her back."

"Um - have you been able to rule Jeff out as a suspect yet?"

"Not entirely. We did get the surveillance recording from the parking lot at the pier, and his truck pulled in there at 10:00 and didn't move until 1:15. So if he did drive up the coast to kill Barkley, he did it in someone else's car."

"He didn't do that."

Max's tone grew gentler. "Off the record? We don't think he did. We've subpoenaed phone records for everyone involved, and we'll get the GPS and confirm his movements. That should clear him. But it'll take a few days to get those."

"Okay. Thanks, Max."

"You're welcome."

That evening, I was just getting ready to leave my office when the phone rang. I didn't recognize the number, but the area code was 703. Northern Virginia. Possibly one of my relatives - so I answered.

A voice that sounded vaguely familiar said, "Jamie?"

"Yes?"

"Hey, it's Tanner."

Shit. My no-good cousin Tanner, my Uncle Dennis's third son, the Brodie black sheep. I hadn't spoken to Tanner since our Uncle Doug's sixtieth birthday, nearly six years ago.

My immediate thought was, *He's going to ask for money.*

My second thought was, *How the hell did he find out so fast?*

"Hey, Tanner. How are you?"

"Oh, you know. Takin' one day at a time."

Tanner had a long history of substance abuse. Last I'd heard, his stepfather had gotten him a low-level job in a bank after Tanner had been released from rehab last year.

I said, "Are you working?"

"Um, not at the moment. I was working at a bank, but they got bought out by a bigger company and I got laid off."

I had no idea if that was the case and didn't really care. "Oh, too bad."

"Nah, it's all good. It gives me a chance to go back to school. I need to finish my business degree, then I won't be one of the ones that gets laid off when shit like that happens."

"Sounds like a plan." I shut down my computer, gathered my belongings, locked my office and headed for the stairs.

"Yeah. But here's the thing…"

I thought, *Here it comes*.

"I can't get a loan. My credit rating's too bad, and Dad won't cosign."

Of course he wouldn't. Uncle Dennis had bailed Tanner out too many times. I wasn't surprised that he was over it. I said, "What about your mom?"

"Same deal. Cliff won't let her."

Cliff was Tanner's stepfather. He was no dummy either. I said, "You should get a job at Starbucks or someplace that will pay for your education."

"Shit, there's no way I could work and go to school at the same time. You know I'm not smart like the rest of you. I need to be able to concentrate on school."

Yeah, right. I reached the bus stop and leaned against the shelter. Time to get to the point. "Tanner, if you're asking for money, the answer is no."

He laughed, but I heard the tension in his voice. "Dude, c'mon. We're family."

"Exactly. I *know* you. I talk to your brothers all the time. I know what you'd do with any money you got, and it ain't paying tuition."

His tone changed to something harder. "Fuck, man, you've got millions. What're you gonna do with all that money that you can't throw a little of it my way?"

The bus arrived, and I climbed onto it. I hissed softly, "It's none of your business what I'm gonna do with it. I don't even have it yet, and when I do, I'm not throwing any of it anywhere. I'm especially not gonna watch any of it turn into white powder and disappear up your nose."

Tanner was pissed. "Fuck you, faggot. I won't forget this."

"Same to you, dude." I hung up.

I was getting off the bus when my phone rang again. This time it was Kevin.

He said, "You'll never believe who just called me."

"Our dear cousin Tanner?"

"Okay, so you would believe it. He called you first?"

"Yeah, about a half hour ago. What story did he tell you?"

"That he has gambling debts, and if he doesn't pay they'll break his legs."

"Ha. That's more likely to be true. He told me he needed money for school. When I told him no, he called me a faggot and sort of vaguely threatened me."

Kevin made a sound of disgust. "I laughed at him. Told him that getting his legs broken would build character. He said, 'Fuck you,' and hung up on me. How did he threaten you?"

"He just said, 'I won't forget this.' I said neither would I. Think he'll call Jeff?"

"Probably. But Jeff won't talk to him."

"Maybe Val will answer the phone. That should be entertaining."

Kevin laughed. "You know, I haven't talked to Uncle Dennis for a while. I think I'll give him a call."

"Sounds like a good idea. Did you find out anything about the clothing labels on your Jane Doe?"

"Yeah, it's a private label for a store that's only located in the South, as far west as Texas. But that doesn't help much. Jane Doe could have moved here from a southern state and brought her clothes with her. Or she could be a tourist."

"Did Jon get anything from the witness?"

"Just a vague description of a dark-colored car that didn't fit the neighborhood."

"In other words, no."

"Exactly."

I reached the walk leading to our front door at the same time as Susan Portman and Max O'Brien. I said, "Detectives. What can we do for you?"

Max said, "Sorry to show up at dinnertime. We were hoping to pick your brain about a few things."

"Sure." I unlocked the door and led the cops into the house. "Can I get you anything to drink?"

Max said, "No, thanks."

I heard Pete walking around upstairs and called up to him. "Pete? The detectives are here."

"*Oh.*" Pete zipped downstairs. "Hi."

Susan said, "We're sorry to show up at dinnertime."

Pete said, "It's okay, it's in the crock pot. How can we help you?"

Susan reached into her jacket pocket and took out her notebook. "We wanted to get your impressions on a few things. We have a list of potential suspects."

I said, "Aren't we all potential suspects?"

"Of course. But we've been able to rule some of you out. You and Dr. Ferguson, for instance."

I said, "And my brother Kevin and my dad, I hope."

"Yes." Susan consulted her list. "Of all the family members affected by the accident that Barkley caused, we have the following. Your dad was with his lady friend that night. Your brother Jeff hasn't been ruled out yet, although as Max told you, we do have surveillance footage of the parking lot."

I said, "Does your footage show him leaving and coming back to the truck?"

"Yes, and it coincides with the times that he claimed to be there. Not that he couldn't have borrowed a car from someone else and driven to LA, but it seems unlikely."

"Good."

Susan nodded. "Kevin was in the Valley with his girlfriend, and has a receipt from a gas station at about the time of Barkley's death. You and Dr. Ferguson have only each other as an alibi for the approximate time of death, but you do have that receipt from Vons, and we have surveillance from that parking lot as well, so we know you were there."

I said, "I didn't kill him."

Susan said, "For what it's worth, I don't think you did."

Pete said, "I'm glad to hear that."

Susan smiled a little and consulted her notes again. "Belinda Marcus, obviously, can't pull a trigger. Her husband plays poker with some of his Marine buddies on Saturday nights, and Josh often goes down to spend the evening with his mother, which he did on the night in question. Brian Marcus's friends confirmed that he was with them at Camp Pendleton from 8 pm to midnight that night."

Pete said, "By which time Barkley was already dead."

"Yes." Susan flipped a page.

Max said, "You met Josh Marcus, right? What was your impression of him?"

I considered. "I didn't get much of an impression other than it seemed he was trying to ingratiate himself with the attorney."

"Okay." Susan went back to the list. "Karen Marcus Fornari was confirmed to be on an overnight Girl Scout camping trip in Colorado."

Pete said, "Had anyone else visited Barkley in prison?"

Susan grinned. "Now that's an interesting question. Other than the Doctors Brodie, Barkley also had several visits in the past year from Tony Jemison and his daughter Jenna McCune. Although Tony and Jenna both have alibis."

Pete said, "Why was Jemison visiting Barkley?"

Max said, "He's taken up Buddhism. The whole Zen – forgiveness thing."

I said, "Drew doesn't have an alibi, though."

"No, he doesn't. He's still a suspect."

Max said, "We're checking his phone GPS too. See if we can prove where he was. Or wasn't."

Susan checked her notebook. "That brings us to the Crabtrees."

Pete asked, "Did you find out when Marie got into town?"

"Yes, she took the red eye from Atlanta and got here early Saturday. And she flew into LAX, not San Diego."

I said, "Why would she do that if her intent was to visit Belinda Marcus?"

Susan pointed her pen at me. "Exactly."

Pete said, "Were you able to rule out the other Crabtrees?"

Max said, "Two of them. Finn, the son, lives in Boston and is a registered nurse at Mass General. He was on shift that night."

I said, "I thought his name was Asher?"

"That's his first name. He goes by his middle name. We also ruled out Rick Crabtree, who says he put Marie on the plane at Hartsfield and went home. We have no evidence that he traveled to California, and he was seen by his next door neighbors the following morning getting the newspaper at the end of his driveway."

I said, "Which leaves the daughter."

"Alexandra. Goes by Alex. She lives in Miami, but her phone's off. We're still trying to track her down."

Pete said, "Did Barkley make any enemies in prison?"

Susan answered. "Not according to the officials at Folsom. He kept his head down, spent most of his time studying, taking classes online, reading in the library."

"Any other visitors of interest?"

"He almost never got visitors at all. He got a couple of visits from a guy who taught one of his certificate classes, who was supposedly going to help him get a job here in LA. Patrick Gomez.

He's coming into the station tomorrow for an interview. Barkley was also visited about once every two or three months by Gordon Smith."

I asked, "What about Barkley's girlfriend? Kate Bianchi? She lived in a near-vegetative state for twelve years after the accident, then she died. Are any of her family members still around?"

Max said, "Her parents are both deceased, within the past couple of years, of natural causes. She had a brother, Vincent Bianchi. We're not having much luck finding him either."

Susan referred back to her list. "So here's the final list of suspects that can't confirm their whereabouts on Saturday night. Jeff Brodie, Drew Jemison, Marie Crabtree, Alex Crabtree, Vincent Bianchi."

I said, "Where was Gordon Smith?"

Susan's eyebrows went up in interest. "We haven't spoken to him. Why do you ask?"

I shrugged. "Just a thought. He and old man Barkley were tight. Smith's paralegal told my attorney that Barkley wouldn't deal with anyone in the office but Smith. Smith told us that he'd tried to talk Barkley out of changing his will, but he'd gone ahead and done it."

"What would his motive be?"

"I don't know."

"Hm." Portman made a note. "We'll talk to him."

Pete said, "What about the tenth beneficiary? Jennelle Shifflett?"

Max frowned. "We don't know who she is. We can't find her. There's no record of anyone by that name in California."

I said, "Gordon Smith would know where she is."

Susan said, "Yes, he would."

When Susan and Max left, Pete dished up our chicken and dumplings, and I finally had an opportunity to tell him about the events of the day, ending with Tanner's call. He shook his head. "How did he find out about it?"

"Who knows? The will is public record, but how would he have known to look it up? Someone in the family must have said something."

Pete frowned. "I thought no one in the family spoke to him."

"His mother does. Or he may have overheard a conversation between his mom and one of the other boys."

"Does his mom stay in touch with Will and Henry?"

"Yeah, she was their stepmother for several years. They've remained on good terms."

"Do you have any other long-lost relatives to come out of the woodwork?"

"There are more distant cousins on Sarge's side of the family, but as far as I know, they're all upstanding citizens."

"Well." Pete stabbed a bite of chicken and examined it. "Let's hope that's the last you'll hear from Tanner."

I spent the rest of the evening answering the phone. The first call was from my Uncle Dennis.

I said, "Hey, Uncle Denny, how are you?"

"Hey, yourself. I'm fine. I hear you got a call from Tanner."

"Yes, sir."

"I'm sorry about that."

"Oh, you don't have to apologize."

"I think it's my fault that Tanner found out about the will, though. I mentioned it to Tyler, who probably told his mother, and Tanner must have heard somehow."

"It's okay. Wills are public record. It's hard to keep news like that hidden."

Dennis snorted. "Tanner's a disgrace. I've told him he can come to me for anything *but* money. Needless to say I haven't heard from him for months."

"When I was at Doug's last spring, Will told me that Cliff had gotten Tanner a job at his bank."

"He did, and that lasted for about six months. The moron got caught taking money out of the till. Cliff fired him on the spot, and rightly so."

"Ha. He told me the bank had been taken over and he'd been laid off."

Dennis laughed. "The gambling debts story that he gave Kevin could be true, although I don't know that for certain. He may just want it for drugs."

"That's what I figured."

Dennis sighed. "I don't know where we went wrong with that kid. Marilyn was a good mom, and Cliff was a good stepdad. They didn't spoil him or let him get away with any shit."

I said, "It wasn't anyone's fault. Tyler turned out fine, and he had the same parents, right?"

"I suppose. So what are you going to do with the money?"

"Hang on to most of it, I guess. I've been teaching extra classes for the history department, and I'll stop doing that. We're going to build a place near Pete's brother, so we have somewhere to go when California falls into the sea."

He laughed. "And now you can fly first class when you travel."

"Right. And come see the family more often, I hope."

"That'd be great. Anyway, I just wanted to tell you that I was sorry Tanner bothered you. I'll try to make sure you don't hear from him again."

The second phone call I got was from Val, who was laughing when I answered. "Hey, Val. What's funny?"

"Oh my God, I just got off the phone with your loser cousin."

"Wonderful. What sob story did he give you?"

"First he demanded to speak to Jeff, who refused to talk to him. So then he appealed to me. Said he had gotten laid off and had a line on a job doing construction but had to have a hernia operation before he could get hired."

"Ha. That's awesome. He told me he needed money to go back to school, and he told Kevin he needed money for gambling debts."

"Are any of those true?"

"Maybe the gambling debts. I just talked to his dad. What did you say to him?"

"I told him to apply for Medicaid. I also told him that we had two mortgages, two kids to send to college and three parents that could need nursing homes someday, so he was wasting his breath."

"What did he say?"

"He grumbled and whined a little, tried to appeal to my motherly instincts. I told him I didn't have any."

I laughed. "You rock, Val."

I could almost hear her grin through the phone. "Of course I do."

My final call of the evening was from my cousin Tyler, Tanner's younger brother and the other gay member of our clan. "Jamie! Oh my *God*, Dad said Tanner called you to ask for money!"

"Yep. Are you surprised?"

"Kind of. I wouldn't have thought he had the balls. I guess he's more desperate than I thought."

"What's his real problem?"

"I haven't spoken to him for ages. I think he asked Henry for money not long ago. He told him it was for gambling debts."

"That's what he told Kevin too. Maybe it is true."

"Maybe, or he might just be on drugs again. I don't know, and I don't care."

"I hear ya. How's the wedding planning coming?" Tyler and his boyfriend had been engaged for nearly a year and weren't getting married for another year.

"Oh my *God*. We thought we had a caterer chosen, then she said she couldn't do gluten-free, so now we have to find someone else."

"Gluten-free is disgusting, Ty."

"I know, but Blair is gluten-sensitive. We're going to have regular food too, but several of the guests have issues."

"I bet they do."

He giggled. "*Stop* it. What about you? Are you even *doing* any wedding planning?"

"Not much. We've picked a date and a location, and Neil's going to do the ceremony and host the reception."

"What location?"

"Where we got engaged, on the hiking trail at Eagle Rock in Topanga State Park. I'll be the one in hiking boots and a flannel shirt."

Tyler giggled again. "Oh my *God*. You're *so* butch."

I laughed. "You're a mess, Ty."

He laughed too. "Oh God, don't I know it. Listen, Blair's making faces at me, so I'd better go. Take care."

"You too."

Pete looked up at me from the desk, amused. "How's Tyler's wedding planning coming along?"

"They're having trouble finding a caterer who will do gluten-free."

"Oh, for God's sake. Does the boyfriend actually need gluten-free?"

"I doubt it. I think he's just trendy." I went to Pete and stood behind him, rubbing his shoulders. "Tyler says we're butch, too."

"Then it must be true. Maybe we should grow beards for the wedding."

I snickered. "I think we're developing a theme."

Tuesday, April 21

After I dismissed my class on Tuesday, I walked over to the UCLA credit union to meet Pete. We did all of our banking there, and I wanted to get our new account set up and ready to accept the money when it came.

We went in and were guided to a customer service rep named Gary. We explained what we needed, and I handed him the paper on which I'd written the amount of the impending deposit. He read it and nodded. "Thirty-seven-plus thousand. We can certainly help you with that."

"Um - no." I pointed to the figure. "Thirty-seven-plus million."

Gary read the figure again and sucked in a breath, mouth open. "Oh. My." He blinked a couple of times, struggling to hide his shock and delight. "Do you have a financial adviser?"

"We do."

"Good." Gary blinked a couple more times, trying to regain his composure. "I'm sure he or she has suggested that you make no major decisions about using the money for at least a year."

I said, "We haven't actually spoken to her yet, but that's our intention."

"How soon are you getting the money?"

"A couple of weeks."

"The thing to do, then, is to have the deposit go into your existing account. At that time, come in and we'll set up CDs. Our best rate is 1.6% for a 60-month CD, with a minimum deposit of $100,000. You'll want to buy a series of CDs with different maturity rates, so that you'll always have one coming available in six months. Then you can either let it roll over, or move some of it to your regular account so it's accessible."

I nodded. "Makes sense. So we don't actually have to do anything now? Just give the attorney our existing account number?"

"That's right. When the money becomes available in your account, come back and we'll set you up." He handed us his card.

"Thank you. Can I have another card? My brother does his banking here, and he's in the same situation."

"Good God." Gary's equanimity was evaporating again at the news that they'd be receiving *another* $38 million. "Of course. Tell him to see me when the payment is made." He stood and shook our hands. "I'm sorry for your loss."

"What?"

"Your family member who made these bequests. I'm sorry."

"*Oh.*" Pete laughed; Gary gave him an odd look. I said, "It wasn't a family member. It was - it's a long story."

"Ah. Well, then." Gary smiled. "I'll see you in a couple of weeks."

Pete came back to the office with me and did some grading while I finished out my workday. We were walking to the car when Kevin called. "Here's your daily update on the Barkley case. Max tried to call Marie Crabtree again, and she's not answering her phone."

"Did they get the GPS information back yet?"

"No, it's too soon. They did find Barkley's motel room and found a blood pool there, just a few days old."

"But I thought Barkley was shot where he was found."

"He was."

"So whose blood is it?"

"Don't know. They're testing it."

"And the motel didn't *report* this?"

Kevin snorted. "It wasn't exactly an upscale place. Rooms by the hour, you know what I mean? They found the blood the next day, but since no one had complained or heard anything, they just figured someone got a bloody nose. They were making arrangements to replace the carpet."

"A bloody nose? Seriously?"

"Clearly the motel manager didn't want the cops poking around too thoroughly. Let's just say the place is well known to Pacific Division. But Max said there was far too much blood for it to have been a bloody nose."

I sighed. "This is getting complicated."

"No shit."

"Did they talk to Barkley's friend? He was going to help him find a job."

"Yeah. Patrick Gomez. He's an addictions counselor, got to know Gavin when he taught one of the classes in his certificate program. He met Gavin at the bus stop Wednesday evening, bought him dinner, gave him enough money for a pay as you go cell phone and told Gavin to call him the next day. Then he dropped him off at the motel. On Thursday, Gavin called Gomez in the afternoon, and Gomez told him that he'd set up an interview for him Monday. He said Gavin was excited about that. That was the last he heard from him."

"Where's Gavin's cell phone?"

"Missing."

"What about your Jane Doe?"

"Nothing new. We're going to expand our search for missing persons tomorrow. We sent the bullet for ballistics; maybe we can link the gun to someone if it was used in a previous crime."

"Thanks for the update. Hey, listen, Pete and I went to the credit union this afternoon, and the guy we talked to said to put the money in our existing accounts when it comes. Then he'll set up CDs for us. We can't do it now; the minimum deposit is a hundred grand."

Kevin huffed a laugh. "Yeah, can't do that now."

A thought occurred to me. "You have an account that's separate from Abby's, right? For the inheritance?"

"Way ahead of you, short stuff. I've been keeping half of the money from working for Mel in my own account from the beginning."

"Good. What's going on with her?"

"She's been spending the night at Amy's most of the time. She says it's because Amy needs help now that the twins are walking. I didn't get into it with her."

"She hasn't said anything about Sean?"

"Nope. I've started gathering ATM receipts. She has a bad habit of leaving them lying around. She's been withdrawing an extra hundred bucks a week for the past four months."

"Out of your joint account?"

"Yeah."

I sighed. "Gather your evidence, detective."

His voice was grim. "You bet."

Wednesday, April 22

Wednesday morning, Kevin called. "The GPS records are back. Jeff's phone showed he was at the Oceanside Pier when he said he was. He's clear."

"*Excellent*. What about the others?"

"Drew Jemison was cleared too. His phone never left his house, and he was actually on the phone with various people most of the night, until about 2:30 am. If he killed Gavin, he would have had to do it while he was talking on the phone."

"What about Alexandra Crabtree?"

"She's missing."

"Missing? Like missing persons missing?"

"Yeah. Susan talked to the brother again. Finn. Alex was last seen Thursday at work. She told them she was taking a long weekend and would be back Monday. She didn't come back. She also hasn't been answering her phone since Friday, which is the last time anyone spoke with her. The brother and employer both said this is extremely unlike her. She's always been a model employee, and her brother talks to her every other day or so. The brother and the boss put their heads together, and the boss filed a missing persons report."

"But she lives in Florida. That can't have anything to do with Gavin's murder."

"Well - Susan and Max got the GPS on Alexandra's phone, too. She arrived in LA on Friday."

"Uh oh."

"Exactly. Her GPS showed her in Venice, very near Gavin's motel. Then she apparently walked to the end of the pier and disappeared."

"Or she threw her phone in the water so she couldn't be tracked."

"Yep. And - the last person she was known to have spoken to was her mother, who followed her to LA the next day."

"Oy. This is getting messy."

"Indeed. Susan is having the divers look around the end of the pier for a phone. Or a body."

"Speaking of bodies - anything new on your Jane Doe?"

"No. We should get the ballistics back tomorrow. And... we've requested Alex Crabtree's dental records."

I sucked in a breath. "Shit. You think your Jane is Alex?"

He sighed. "Alex is missing. Jane was wearing clothes from a store that's only located in the Southeast. We know Alex came to LA. The general description fits. It's possible."

I considered that. "Her mother couldn't have killed her. She wasn't in LA yet."

"I know. If our ballistics match Susan's, it's possible that Gavin killed her. She was near his motel on Friday night."

"The blood pool in his motel room."

"Yeah."

"So... if Gavin killed Alex, did her mother kill Gavin?"

"I don't know. Susan is requesting a subpoena for Marie Crabtree's phone records." I heard Jon's voice in the background. "Gotta go."

At noon, I took my lunch outside and called my dad while I ate. After we said hello, I asked, "How well did you know Marie Crabtree?"

He sounded surprised. "Why?"

"Just curious."

"Not as well as I knew Belinda or Tracy. Rick Crabtree had just been posted to Pendleton about six months before the accident. Around the time you were born. He and Marie lived next door to Brian and Belinda on base and had become instant friends with Belinda, which is why Marie was with the girls that night."

"Did you get to know her after the accident?"

"Not well. She was hospitalized for a couple of months and in rehab after that. I saw her a few times when we met with the prosecutor during the trial."

"Did you know her husband well?"

"No. What's this about?"

"She was here in LA when Gavin Barkley was killed and lied to the police about it, her daughter is missing now, and she made that weird visit to us. I just wondered what your impressions of her were."

Dad considered for a moment. "Marie never came to the house. I don't think that Julie and she would have been friends if it wasn't for Belinda. I asked Julie about that once, and she said, 'She's an *officer's* wife,' with air quotes and rolling her eyes. I knew what she meant by that."

"Which was what?"

"Pearls and parties." My dad chuckled. "The stereotype of the officer's wife was someone who was mostly concerned with her social status. Even though it was the seventies, a lot of officers' wives seemed to be stuck in the fifties. They'd given up the bouffant hairdos, but they all wore those shirtwaist dresses with low heels and pearls, even when they were at home."

"Like Leave It to Beaver's mom."

"Exactly. And they all played the one-upmanship game with each other when backs were turned, even though they were friendly to each other's faces. Politics were involved, and social standing based on their husbands' rank." He huffed a laugh. "It's one of the reasons I was always glad to be a grunt."

"I'm sure Mom didn't go for that at all."

"Oh, hell, no. Like I said, she and Marie wouldn't have been friends without Belinda as the go-between."

"But Belinda was an officer's wife."

"She was different. Belinda liked everyone. You never saw a better soul than Belinda. She never met a stranger. She lived next door to Marie, so she helped her ease into Pendleton society out of kindness."

I said, "Marie was the least affected by the accident, but I'm sure she had a hard row to hoe."

"She did. After rehab, she had to have a good bit of reconstructive surgery on her legs – plastic surgery, skin grafts. It had to be a long, painful process."

"She was wearing a long skirt when she came to see us. I guess if she has a lot of scarring, she doesn't show her legs."

"Probably not." Dad was silent for a moment. "I know the police are considering old man Barkley's heirs as their primary suspects, but the people with the strongest desire for vengeance are Marie, Belinda, Tony and me."

"You and Tony have alibis, Brian Marcus and Rick Crabtree have alibis, and Belinda can't pull a trigger."

"I know." Dad's voice was grim. "Which leaves Marie."

I said, "Barkley was killed two days after he was released from prison. Whoever killed him may have planned for that exact event, whether he got out on parole or served his full term."

Dad said, "The Klingons were right. 'Revenge is a dish best served cold.'"

I was back at my desk when my office phone rang, a number with a 949 area code - Irvine - that I didn't recognize. "Young Research Library, can I help you?"

"Jamie? It's Drew Jemison."

Whoa. "Hi, Drew. What's up?"

"I was wondering if you'd like to get together for a drink. I was going to call you before, but then Barkley was killed - I didn't think I should contact you while we were under suspicion."

"Good thinking. Sure, I'd like to get together."

"I know it's short notice, but this evening would be good for me."

"Um - yeah, I can do that. Is it okay if my fiancé comes too?"

"Sure."

"Where do you want to meet?"

"I live in Downey. But I don't mind coming to Westwood."

"No, no, we'll meet you someplace closer than that. Downtown, at least."

We met Drew Jemison at a Mexican restaurant in Silver Lake. He slouched into the booth across from me and lifted his Dos Equis to us. "Semper Fi."

I said, "Semper Fi." We drank.

Drew didn't seem to know how to begin. I said, "So, you've been cleared. Good news."

"Yeah. So has Jeff."

We sat for a minute. I said, "I don't remember my mom."

"No, you wouldn't." Drew smiled slightly, and for a minute I could imagine from the expression on his face what he must have looked like as a little boy. "I remember her. She was great. Used to bring us latex gloves from the hospital to use as balloons."

I laughed. "She and your mom were best friends."

"Yeah." He smiled again. "My mom had been a nurse, but when Jenna and I came along she wanted to be a stay at home mom. That's why we lived on base. It was cheaper."

"Do you remember much about what happened after the accident?"

"All of it. The accident blew our family apart." He looked up at me. "My dad always said that your family pulled in the wagons. Ours disintegrated."

"Belinda Marcus told me that your dad had remarried."

"Yeah, and he did it too quickly. He couldn't face raising us alone. He didn't know what to do. He already knew Sandy – my stepmother – and they were married right after the trial was over."

"She had kids of her own?"

"A boy and two girls. I got along okay with the boy, although we had our fights, but my sister hated the girls. *Hated* them. And there were two of them, so they were always ganging up on her. And my dad didn't do anything about it." Drew frowned, turning his beer bottle on the table. "He started drinking. The Marines finally told him that he either needed to shape up or get out. He decided to get out while he could still get an honorable discharge."

"What did he do in the Marines?"

"Motor pool. Engine repair. He went to work for a mechanic in San Diego, but he was still drinking. He and Sandy fought all the time. The marriage lasted for six years before they split up. By that time my sister and I were teenagers, so we could manage on our own. We ran the house and took care of everything while Dad stayed drunk all the time."

"You had to become adults before you should have."

"Yeah." Drew took a drink and set his bottle on the table with a thump. "Builds character, right?"

It was a rhetorical question. I said, "Did your dad get straightened out?"

That produced a smile. "He did... about ten years ago. I guess he woke up one morning, hung over, and said, 'Fuck this.' He became a vegetarian, sold our house and bought the farm up in Oregon and started growing organic vegetables." He gave us a sideways look. "And weed."

Pete huffed a laugh. I said, "Ah. Income."

Drew grinned. "Yeah. He sells his vegetables at the farmer's market, but most of his income comes from the other crop."

Who was I to judge? "It's a living."

"He went the hippie route, I guess. Back to the sixties, before everything went wrong."

"Would he have blamed Gavin Barkley for everything going wrong?"

"No. One of the other things that he did was become Buddhist. He always blamed himself, and the Buddhism seems to have helped him accept the responsibility and move on."

Pete said, "Why would he blame himself?"

"For encouraging my mom to drive that night. She didn't like driving at night, but he knew your mom couldn't drive because you all only had one car, and Belinda Marcus didn't have a drivers' license. And he didn't trust Marie Crabtree."

"Why?"

He shrugged. "He never said. He didn't like her much, I know that. So he'd told my mom to take the car and go have a good time."

I said, "I don't think it would have mattered what car they were in."

"Yeah, but if my mom hadn't been driving, she and your mom would have been in the back seat. It would have been them who lived. Besides, the Crabtrees had some honkin' big car. The damage wouldn't have been as bad."

I said, "Where does your sister live?"

"Eugene, Oregon. She works in the admissions office at the University of Oregon, and Dad's place is not far. She's got kids, so she wanted them to grow up near Dad. And her husband's from Portland, so they're closer to his family there too."

Pete said, "What do you do?"

Drew looked a little embarrassed. "I'm a groundskeeper at UC-Irvine."

I said, "Oh, cool. That's an attractive campus. You all do a great job."

That pleased him. "Thank you. I enjoy being outside. I'm not an office person." He smiled, and I saw the little boy in his face again. "I'm like my dad, I guess."

"Are you close to your dad now?"

"Yeah. We talk a couple of times a week."

I raised my bottle. "Here's to our dads."

"Amen." Drew drained his beer. "I'm glad Gavin Barkley is dead."

I hadn't realized it until that moment, but so was I. I said, "Me, too."

Drew cocked his head and smiled. "You don't remember me, do you?"

"No. I was surprised that Jeff did."

"My mom babysat you guys when your mom went back to work. I was in first grade, but we'd keep you all entertained when we got home from school."

Pete said, "You must have been patient to throw a Nerf football with a toddler."

Drew grinned. "He was a cute kid. Mom had her hands full with you and Kevin, so I didn't mind entertaining Jeff."

I said, "I was just a baby."

"Yeah, but you were crawling. You and Kevin were into everything." Drew smiled sadly. "Those were happy days. Good memories. Then the accident happened, and we never saw you all again except for the trial."

"Do you remember the trial?"

"Some of it. I remember walking into the courtroom."

"You were so young, I'm surprised they let you testify."

"It wasn't really testimony." Drew sighed. "They mostly just asked me about my mom. About the things we did together."

"That had to be traumatic."

"It doesn't seem like it now. Maybe because what came after was so disruptive."

Pete said, "You made it through, though."

Drew smiled. "Yeah." He nodded to me. "We all did."

Thursday, April 23

The California Psychological Association annual conference was being held in San Diego Thursday through Sunday, and Pete had registered to go. He'd be staying with my dad - after our experience at my library conference, Pete had chosen to stay out of the hotel. It wasn't a good time for me to take off, so I didn't go with him. I'd see him Saturday, at Lauren Fortner's office - we'd finally gotten our appointment with her for our first dose of financial advice.

We got up early and took a quick run, then Pete wolfed down a bowl of cereal. His first event began at ten, and he wanted to be on the road by seven. I kissed him goodbye at the Jeep. "Talk to you this evening."

"Right." He kissed me back a little longer this time. "Stay out of trouble."

"Who, me?"

He laughed and drove off. I headed for the bus stop with a smile on my face.

The day was uneventful, and I was able to catch up on a few things I'd gotten behind on due to all the phone conversations I'd been having. Pete called at about 5:30; I was still at my desk. I said, "Hey, how was your day?"

"Good. The Neuropsychology Institute was great information. And I saw Dr. Bibbins. She was at the Couples Therapy Institute."

"I'm glad to hear that. Maybe she'll learn some new tactics for us."

"Yeah. And I saw Bryn."

"Ah." Bryn Davies was a young guy we'd met in a gay bar in Oxford last summer, a psychology student at Magdalen College. He and Pete had experienced an immediate connection; I could almost see the sparks fly between them. Bryn had emailed Pete a few days later, ostensibly about psychology - but I'd thought it was more than that on Bryn's part. He'd emailed Pete back in November to tell him he was attending this conference.

I said, "Did he seek you out?"

"I think so. He was outside the Neuropsychology Institute meeting room when it let out."

"He's stalking you."

Pete sighed. "I don't think he is. I think he's just hoping I've become single."

"Did you spend any time with him?"

"Absolutely *not*. I had lunch with Aaron and Elliott." Elliott was the assistant chair of Pete's department. "I'll be hanging out with them during the day and going straight to your dad's after the meetings are over."

"Okay."

"I'm serious, Jamie. I'm avoiding him."

"I know. Just - watch out."

Kevin called about a half hour later. "When are you going home?"

"In a few minutes. Why?"

"We're both on our own tonight. Want to get something to eat?"

"Sure. What's Abby doing?"

"Spending the night at Amy's."

"Why don't you spend the night with me? Go home and pack a bag then come pick me up. You'll be closer to work tomorrow."

"Okay. Makes sense."

When Kevin picked me up, we went through the In-N-Out drive-thru and got burgers - a rare treat for me these days, since Pete had eschewed red meat after his dad's heart attack. We spent the evening watching TV. At about ten, I pulled out the sofa bed for Kevin, made sure he had everything he needed and went to bed.

I texted Pete. *You still up?*

Yeah.

Kevin's spending the night.
Good. I'm in bed reading.
I'm going to take a shower and go to bed.
Think of me in the shower.
Ha. I intend to.

Friday, April 24

When I got up the next morning, Kevin was sitting at the kitchen table on the phone. "Okay. Yeah, that's fine. Perfect. See you there." He hung up and said, "Ballistics are back."

"Good morning to you too. What did they show?"

"The bullet in our Jane Doe and the bullet in Gavin's head were both fired from the gun in Gavin's hand. Susan's put a rush on the DNA sample from the motel room. If that blood matches Jane, then it's looking better than Gavin killed her."

"And that she's Alex Crabtree."

"Maybe. We should have the dental comparison later today." He got up and started looking in cabinets. "Where's your cereal?"

"Here." I handed him a box of raisin bran. "Bowls are right above your head."

"Thanks." He poured cereal and milk and began to eat. "It's a good thing I stayed here. Susan and Max want to have a powwow first thing, down at Pacific."

"Have you heard from Abby?"

"Yeah, she called and woke me up about an hour ago. She was on her way to work."

"That early? Have you been seeing overtime pay in your account?"

"Nope."

My phone buzzed with a text from Pete. *You up?*

Yep. Having cereal with Kevin. Sleep well?

Okay. Missed you.

Me too. Have fun today. But not too much.

Ha. Love you too.

Kevin said, "Is Pete going to be able to come to the meeting at Lauren's with the conference?"

"Yeah. His sessions run from 8:30 to noon and from 4:00 to 5:30." Our meeting was scheduled for 1:00.

"You spending tomorrow night at Dad's?"

"Yeah."

"Cool." He slurped the rest of his milk from his bowl and hopped to his feet. "Gotta hit the shower."

My work day was uneventful and productive. I headed for the bus stop at five, planning to pick up takeout Indian food, then pack for my overnight stay at Dad's tomorrow. I was nearly home when I got a text from Kevin. *You home?*

Almost.

Can I come over?

Sure.

OK be there in a few.

He must have been close by. Five minutes later, the doorbell rang. Kevin was in jeans and a t-shirt, looking morose. I said, "What's up? Did Abby have to work this evening?"

"No." He came into the house and went to the kitchen, folding himself into one of the dining chairs, and sniffed my Indian food. "Go ahead and eat."

"Have you eaten?"

"Yeah."

"Want a drink?"

"*Yes.*"

The way he said it made me raise my eyebrows. I took a beer from the fridge and handed it to him; he drained a third of it immediately. I sat down across from him with a bottle of my own. "I assume you're not on call tonight."

"No." Kevin sighed. "Abby's babysitting Amy's kids again. Amy and Tom are having a date weekend or something."

I said, "What else is going on?"

Kevin rubbed his eyes. "Abby's haranguing me to quit my job immediately."

"Why?"

"Because it's dangerous."

I said, "Come on. As a detective you're in almost no danger. Doesn't she know that?"

"Of course she knows it." Kevin sighed again and drained his beer.

I knew how much Kevin loved Abby, in spite of her behavior lately. This had to be awful for him. I retrieved a second beer and handed it to Kevin. "She still hasn't said anything about Sean?"

"Nope." Kevin shook his head. "She'll never admit that voluntarily."

We sat quietly for a minute. I said, "We get the money in two weeks. Something's gotta give."

He took another long drink and set his bottle on the table with a *thunk*. "You're tellin' me."

Kevin had several more beers, and by 8:30 was smashed. I said, "Why don't we get you upstairs?"

"'Kay."

I hauled him up the steps and into the guest room, where I'd already unfolded the sofa bed. He collapsed onto it, fully clothed and looked at me, bleary-eyed. "G'night."

I said, "At least take off your shoes."

"Oh." Kevin kicked off his shoes and let them drop onto the floor. "G'night."

I turned out all the lights in the office then went back downstairs and made sure the house was secure for the night, leaving a nightlight on in the kitchen and on the staircase in case Kevin got up in the night. I checked our supply of aspirin - we had plenty - and set it on the kitchen table. By the time I got back upstairs, Kevin was snoring.

I took my laptop into the bedroom and graded papers for a while, then called Pete. He groaned as I told him about my evening. "This has to end. Do you know how many women would be falling over Kevin to marry him just *because* of this money?"

"I can imagine." I grinned and said, "So - how do *you* feel about marrying a millionaire?"

Pete chuckled. "Pretty damn good. Seriously, though? It doesn't make any difference. 'For richer and for poorer,' right?"

"Do you feel guilty about using the money?"

He considered that for a minute. "Not... guilty, exactly. I do think of it as your money, not ours, but it's part of the entire package that is you, now. I don't mind benefiting from the money, but I don't think of it as mine."

"So the house in Alamogordo – are you not going to think of that as yours?"

Pete said, "No, it's not that. The land and eventual house feels like ours to me. Our house was mine when you moved in, but it's *our* house now, right? I guess it's the abstract money that doesn't feel like mine. When it's converted into something tangible – that will feel like ours. It's hard to explain."

I did my best Groucho imitation. "So you like my entire package, huh?"

He laughed. "Very much."

I was getting into bed when I got a text from Aaron Quinn. *You'd have been proud of Pete today.*

How so?

That young British guy with the crush on him? Pete politely but firmly told him that you two were engaged and showed him the ring. Made it clear that nothing was going to happen between them.

Whoa. He told me he'd seen Bryn, but he didn't tell me what he'd said to him.

I thought not. I asked him about it, and he acted like it was no big deal.

Did he tell you about meeting Bryn?

Yeah. Said you'd had some discussions on your vacation last year.

LOL that's one way to put it. Wonder why he didn't tell me?

Don't know. I suppose he thought it wasn't worth telling.

Do you mind if I ask him about it?

Nope. Tell him I thought you should know.

Will do. Thanks, Aaron. I set my phone aside and thought about what Aaron had said. Pete had dealt with the Bryn issue on his own. He'd come a long way from last summer.

Not much question left about Pete's readiness for marriage.

I went to sleep with a smile on my face.

Saturday, April 25

The next morning, I woke up gradually, enjoying the feeling of horizontality. I was thinking about going for a run when my phone vibrated. I picked it up to see that it was Abby.

Uh oh. I sat up. "Hey, Abs."

Her voice was strained. "Why are you whispering?"

"Because it's seven in the morning, and Kevin's still asleep."

"His phone is off. I've been trying to reach him for over an hour."

"Is there something wrong?"

"No. I just didn't know where he was."

"He came over last night."

Abby's voice tightened. "Great. I suppose he told you we've been fighting about the money."

"Um – well, he didn't use the word fighting."

"I knew it. I knew he'd go running to you."

I sighed. "Abby, he didn't come running to me. He's confused and wanted to talk it over with someone who knows you. He doesn't understand your attitude toward the money. Neither do I."

"There's nothing to understand. Money like this puts a strain on relationships. That concerns me. I don't want it to come between us."

I decided to be blunt. "Sounds to me like it already has."

She was silent for a minute. "I suppose you and Pete are handling this just fine."

"The inheritance isn't a source of friction for us, no. Maybe you should talk to Val."

"Why? She wants the money."

"Yeah, but Jeff didn't. They had words. Maybe she can clarify things for you."

"I'm not the one who needs clarification."

I sighed again. "Abs, I think you are."

A moment of tense silence, then a clipped, "Fine."

Oh, God. *Fine* with Abby meant anything but. I said, "Do you want Kevin to call you?"

"No. The kids will be up soon, and I won't be able to talk. I just wanted to know where he was."

"And that he was okay."

"What do you mean?"

"You care enough about him to want to make sure he wasn't lying dead in a ditch somewhere."

"Yeah, sure." I heard a screech in the background. "Shit. Gotta go."

I clicked off and sat there thinking for a minute, then tiptoed next door to check on Kevin. He was still breathing, lying on his stomach, his face smushed into his pillow. We didn't have to be in Oceanside until 1:00; I could let him sleep a little longer.

I went for a long run down to the beach, quiet on an early Saturday morning, and stopped for bagels on the way home. When I opened the front door, it was nearly 8:30, and I heard the shower in the guest bathroom running.

I made tea, sorted out bagels and cream cheese on the kitchen table and began to eat. In a few minutes, the shower stopped and Kevin came downstairs, only as far as the landing. "Does Pete have a clean t-shirt I can borrow?"

"Yeah. You need briefs?"

Kevin made a face. "Not used ones, dude."

"I think he has some new ones."

I went to our bedroom and found a shirt, socks and briefs for Kevin and went back downstairs. When he joined me, he didn't look too bad, but he squinted when the light from the big living room windows hit his eyes. "Where's the aspirin?"

"Right here." I handed it to him. "You hungry?"

"Not very."

"You should eat anyway."

Kevin made a face. "Okay, but I don't want cream cheese. Got any jelly?"

I found a jar of strawberry preserves that Val had made, and Kevin managed to eat a bagel. He took his aspirin with a Coke and leaned back. I said, "Feeling a little more human?"

"Yeah. Thanks for letting me crash here."

"Any time. Listen – Abby called a couple of hours ago."

"A couple of hours ago? Did she wake you up?"

"No, I was already awake."

"Was she pissed?"

"A little. More worried, I think. But…" I recounted our conversation.

Kevin groaned. "Great. Abso-fuckin'-lutely great. Do you think she'll call Val?"

"No."

He huffed a laugh. "If she does, I'd like to be a fly on the wall for that conversation."

I said, "Speaking of conversations, something's occurred to me. Susan and Max aren't having any luck connecting with Gordon Smith, right?"

"Right."

"We may know someone else who knows Smith."

Kevin looked confused. "Who?"

"Robbie."

Robbie Harrison was a childhood friend; he'd been my friend with benefits throughout high school. He was a financial planner who specialized in hedge funds and wealthy clients, so he knew a lot of rich folks in the San Diego area. If he didn't know Smith himself, he might know something about him.

Kevin said, "Of course. Let's call him."

I got my phone, found Robbie's number and handed the phone to Kevin, who put the call on speaker. Robbie answered almost immediately. "Jamie?"

"Hey, Robbie, it's Kevin. I'm using Jamie's phone because he already had your number. He's here with me. How are you?"

"Kevin, it's good to hear from you! I'm fine. How about you?"

"I'm good. You still in school?"

"Absolutely. I'm going full time now. I sold the business."

"Did you? That's great."

"Yeah, I made enough from it to stop working until I get my degree." Robbie was in the forensic accounting program at San Diego State. "Anyway - to what do I owe this honor?"

I laughed. Kevin said, "Have you ever heard of a man named Randall Barkley?"

Robbie considered for a minute. "The name's not familiar. Who is he?"

"He died last year. He was the father of the man who killed our mom."

"*Oh*. Why would you think I knew him?"

"He was rich. We thought you might have had him as a client."

"No." Robbie laughed wryly. "I remember names. He wasn't one of mine."

"How about Gordon Smith? He's an attorney in downtown San Diego. Smith, Hendrickson, Delio and Franklin."

"Ah. I don't know Smith personally, but I know Clay Franklin. Not because he was a client; he was my neighbor at the old house. What's this about?"

Kevin said, "Okay, here goes. Randall Barkley was a client of Gordon Smith's. Barkley divided his estate ten ways - among the nine children of the four women involved in the accident, and a tenth person who wasn't involved and whose name no one recognizes. Barkley's son, Gavin, the one who has been in jail all this time for causing the accident and the two deaths, was just paroled a week and a half ago and turned up shot to death three days later. Naturally, the police have been trying to rule all of us out as suspects, thinking of revenge as a motive. But the tenth person wouldn't have had that motive, and the police are having trouble tracking her down. Gordon Smith obviously knows who she is, but he's not exactly cooperating with the police."

"She?"

"Yeah. The name is Jennelle Shifflett."

Robbie said, "Hm. I don't know her."

"There's no reason you should. What we wondered is if you knew someone at the law firm, maybe you could find out if *they* knew her. Would Clay Franklin answer a question like that?"

"I expect he would. Our kids played together and still do; he and I have always gotten along well. Want his number?"

Kevin said, "That would be great."

"Sure. Hang on." A few seconds passed then Robbie said, "Here it is."

I wrote down the number. Kevin said, "Thanks, Robbie. I appreciate it."

"You're welcome. Tell him you're a friend of mine. He'll talk to you."

"Okay." Kevin hung up and dialed the number. He listened for a minute before he whispered "voicemail" to me.

He waited, then said, "Mr. Franklin, this is Detective Kevin Brodie, Los Angeles Police Department Homicide Division." He read off his badge number. "I'd like to speak with you about a case. I'm a friend of Rob Harrison's, and he said you might have some information that we need. Please call me at this number." He read off his own phone number. "Thank you." He hung up and sighed. "Now we'll see if he gets back to me."

He'd barely finished the sentence when his phone rang. Kevin said, "Detective Brodie."

"Detective, this is Clay Franklin. Sorry I didn't answer when you called, but I never answer a number that I don't recognize."

"I don't blame you. Thanks for getting back to me so quickly."

"Sure. What can I do for you?"

"Does the name Jennelle Shifflett mean anything to you?"

There was a moment of surprised silence, then Franklin barked a laugh. "Well, hell. Why do you want to know?"

"We think she might have some information about a murder here in LA."

"You mean Gavin Barkley's murder?"

Interesting. Kevin said, "That's right. Do you know Jennelle Shifflett personally?"

"No. I've never seen her. I know who she is, though."

"And who is that?"

Franklin snorted. "She's Randall Barkley's dirty little secret."

"A mistress?"

"Yep. Back when Mrs. Barkley was still alive and ever since. Right up until the old man died."

"Is she a younger woman?"

"About fifty years younger, according to office gossip."

"She was one of the beneficiaries of Randall Barkley's will."

"I know. Barkley and Gordon Smith argued about it."

"Is Smith going to give you trouble for talking about it?"

Franklin was dismissive. "He can't. I'm a senior partner, same as he is. He and I have equal shares of the firm."

"Mr. Smith has been less than completely cooperative with us."

Franklin made a "pfft" sound. "He's still trying to protect old man Barkley's reputation. From what, I do not know. The asshole's dead, so's his wife. Who cares now?"

Kevin asked, "Would you be able to find contact information for her?"

"I can look right now to see if her contact information is in our database. Hang on." I could hear a keyboard clicking.

Kevin said, "Are you at the office?"

"We're all connected remotely so we can work from home. Let me just pull up this screen." A couple more clicks. "Okay, let's see - Shifflett." He was quiet for a few seconds. "She's not here. Gordon must have her information someplace where only he can see it. You oughta subpoena him."

Kevin said, "It may come to that. One more question. Are you aware of any connection between Gavin Barkley and Ms. Shifflett?"

"No, sorry."

"Okay, Mr. Franklin, I appreciate your cooperation. Would you be willing to give a formal statement to a couple of other detectives, at your convenience?"

"Sure." Franklin laughed. "I was an ADA for twelve years. I love cops. Let me give you my private line at work, and my paralegal will set something up." He recited the numbers.

"Excellent. Thank you, Mr. Franklin. You'll be getting a call from Detective Susan Portman. She's the lead on the case."

"Awesome. I'll look forward to it. Tell Rob I'll see him soon."

"Will do."

Kevin hung up and scrolled through his contacts. "I'd better call Susan."

After Kevin talked to Susan, we hung out at the table for a few minutes, worrying over Kevin's situation with Abby. His phone rang, and he looked at the display. "It's the coroner's office."

"Were you expecting to hear from them?"

"Yep." Kevin answered. "Brodie. Hey, Juanita." He listened for a minute. "Cool. Let me grab a pen."

I dug one out of a drawer with a pad of paper and gave it to him. Kevin said, "Okay, shoot." He wrote for a minute then stopped. "You're sure about this? No, but it ties into a case Pacific has down in Venice. Yeah, the gunshot from the next night. Do you happen to know if Miami-Dade was gonna notify the family? They did? Good.

No, I'll call Portman. Thanks, Juanita." He hung up. "It's confirmed. Our Jane Doe is Alexandra Crabtree."

"*Damn*. I'm not surprised, but I was hoping she was still alive."

"So was I." Kevin turned back to his phone and made another call. "Good *morning*, Detective Eckhoff. We've got an ID on our Benedict vic. Alexandra Crabtree, resident of Coral Gables, Florida. Yes, the very one. No, I'll call Susan. No, Miami-Dade called the family. I know, right? They said the brother is coming to claim the body. Okay, later."

I said, "I'm glad you don't have to do the notification."

"Yeah, me too. Miami-Dade said they'd do it since she lived there."

I cleaned the kitchen while Kevin talked to Susan Portman again. When he hung up, he said, "Susan's going to call Finn Crabtree."

"You said he's coming here?"

"Yeah. He was listed as his sister's next of kin, so he's the one who will have to make the arrangements." Kevin checked the time. "You'd better get moving. We have to leave soon."

Ali's sister, Lauren, was two years older than me. She'd been a math nerd in school and had been a good friend of Jeff's when we were growing up. Lauren had gotten a degree in accounting from San Diego State, passed her CPA exam and opened a practice in Oceanside. A few years later, she'd earned her master's in financial planning. She and her husband, Dustin, owned an office together but split their time so that they overlapped six hours a day. It seemed to work for them.

Her office was not far from my dad's house, in the first floor of a condominium building at the beach. Convenient for all the wealthy oceanfront condo owners. The lettering on the sign was tasteful. "Lauren Fortner, CPA, CFP. Dustin Lemon, MBA, CFP."

We were greeted by the receptionist and shown to the back, where Jeff and Val were sitting with Lauren and Mel at a large round table. Lauren greeted us with hugs. "What can I get you all to drink? I have coffee, water, or Coke."

We all took a drink and sat. Lauren handed Jeff, Kevin and me prepared folders, stuffed with papers. "I made a packet of information for each of you. We'll talk about the basics today, then you can read the details and let me know how to proceed."

I'd brought a notebook and turned to a clean page. "Okay, shoot."

"My first recommendation - the sane thing to do - is to make no major changes at all for a year. Don't quit your jobs, don't sell your houses, don't buy yachts or go to Vegas. The best thing to do is to park the money someplace safe, in CDs for example, spread across several different institutions, and let it sit. Talk about what you'd like to do, give any changes you want to make a *lot* of thought. Then, in a year, I'll get with each of you and see what our next step will be."

Kevin said, "Should we not spend any of it?"

"You should go ahead and splurge on one thing. Mel says that Jamie and Pete are looking at a piece of land in New Mexico to build on. I think it would be fine to go ahead and buy that land. I would recommend waiting to begin the building process, but go ahead and pay cash for the lot you want. Jeff, you mentioned the mortgage on your practice. Paying that off now would be a good splurge. That way you can hire that third veterinarian you need. If you already have a vacation planned and want to upgrade to first class, do it, but don't book any month-long round the world cruises. The idea is to spend just enough to enjoy the benefits of the money, without making any dumb moves."

I said, "We definitely want to avoid dumb moves."

"Absolutely." Lauren began to count on her fingers. "Dumb moves would be: giving a bunch of money to relatives who suddenly come out of the woodwork."

Kevin said, "Like Cousin Tanner."

Jeff snorted. Lauren said, "Right. Dumb move number two: giving any significant amount to charity. We'll do that, if you like, when the time comes, but if you go ahead and do it now in an uncontrolled fashion, you'll get on mailing lists that you'll never get off."

Val said, "Right. No charities yet."

Lauren held up three fingers. "Third dumb move - telling everyone you know. Then word will spread, and you'll be getting requests from people you've never heard of for help. You'll attract media attention and cold calls from real estate agents. You don't want that. Keep the news as close to the vest as you can."

We all nodded somberly.

"Fourth. No self-destructive behavior. Don't gamble. Don't drink more. Don't drive fast. Don't live your life any differently than you have been." She leaned forward, looking each of us in the eye. "You are the same person that you were a month ago. The only thing that's changed is your net worth. We'll make the money work for you, but we can only do that if you don't become a slave to it. Having said that…" She grinned. "Go ahead and make a wish list. Put anything you want on it, no matter how wild. Then prioritize the list. When we reassess in a year, we'll tackle some of those wishes."

We looked around at each other. Jeff said, "Works for me."

I said, "It's going to be hard to keep word from spreading. We've already seen that with our cousin."

"True, but it won't be announced in the media like lottery winners are. If you don't do anything to attract attention, you should be able to keep it under control." Lauren sat back, tapping her pen on the cover of her folder. "The best way to make other people forget that you're rich is to not act like you're rich. Keep living your lives like you have been. In a year, everyone else will have moved on. When you do start using some of the money, no one will notice."

We left Lauren's and walked back to Dad's house, where we'd left our vehicles. Kevin was going back to LA this evening; I'd go home with Pete tomorrow.

When we got to Dad's, he was showing Gabe and Colin how to make hamburger patties. Jeff heated the grill, and we cooked and ate. Jeff, Val and the boys went home, Pete went back to his conference for another session, and Kevin headed back to LA. Dad and I began cleaning up the kitchen. I said, "Kevin and Abby are heading for a breakup."

"I know. He's told me about it."

"Did he tell you she was giving money to Sean? *Their* money?"

"Yeah." Dad shook his head. "I don't understand it."

I said, "I think Abby's oldest sister has been working on her all this time. She's never liked Kevin. She's always told Abby that she shouldn't date a cop. Now Sean's back in the picture... I wouldn't be surprised if Andie called Sean and told him to get in touch with Abby."

"Abby still doesn't realize that Kevin knows about Sean?"

"No."

Dad shook his head. "Unless Abby would agree to counseling, like you and Pete did, I don't see any way forward for them. And it breaks my heart for Kevin. He really thought Abby was the one."

"I know." I wrung out the dish rag and hung it over the faucet. "He's got to stop dating redheads."

Pete's session was over at 5:30, and he was back at Dad's by 6:30. We'd had a late lunch, so we ate salad for dinner. Barb came over, and we talked to her for a while. When she went home, we turned in.

Once we were in bed, out of earshot of Dad, I told Pete about Aaron's text regarding Bryn. "Why didn't you tell me?"

I felt Pete shrug beside me. "I didn't feel like I should brag about finally getting it right."

I squeezed his hand. "I'm proud of you."

He squeezed back. "Thanks."

"Was he crushed by the news?"

Pete huffed a laugh. "If he was, he hid it well. I really don't think he was there for any nefarious purpose. One of the closing session speakers tomorrow is one of the people whose research he's interested in."

"Okay, I'll give him that. He needed to go to a conference, he was interested in hearing this person speak, so he came over with the added bonus that he'd run into you and you might be single by now."

"Could be."

I was nearly asleep when Pete said, "Can I ask a question?"

"Mm. Sure."

"I can't believe I've never asked you this, but it never occurred to me. Why don't you ever visit your mom's grave?"

"I have visited Mom's grave, just not in the past couple of years. She's buried at Arlington National Cemetery."

"Oh. That's a surprise. I would have thought she'd be buried here."

"She was an active duty naval officer and a Vietnam vet. My dad wanted her buried at Arlington."

"We'll visit her grave next summer, won't we?"

"Of course."

Monday, April 27

I'd texted with Kevin a couple of times on Sunday to let him know that we'd gotten back safely. I hadn't heard anything since.

I hoped no news was good news.

I was running late on Monday morning and decided to drive Pete's Jeep to work. My morning was filled with meetings. After my reference shift, I had a research session to lead for an undergraduate history class. When it was over, I left Bunche Hall and headed back to YRL. When I walked past the circulation desk, Lance Scudieri gestured to me. "Dr. Brodie? You have a visitor."

"Oh? Who?"

Lance picked up a scrap of paper he'd written on. "The name was Finn Crabtree. He went into Café 451 to wait."

Finn Crabtree. The younger brother of the murdered Alexandra Crabtree. I glanced at Café 451; it was crowded. "What's he look like?"

"Dishwater blond hair, not too tall, wearing a blue t-shirt and jeans." Lance grinned at me. "He's cute."

"Aha." I grinned back. "Thanks, Lance."

I walked into the cafe and looked around. A guy with rumpled blond hair wearing a blue t-shirt was sitting by himself at a small table. I said, "Finn Crabtree?"

I startled him; he jumped and looked up at me. "Yeah. Are you Jeremy Brodie?"

"Yep. I go by Jamie." I shook his hand. "I'm sorry about your sister."

"Thanks." Finn had his mother's coloring, but his face was less narrow. More open. His eyes were red, and he looked like he hadn't slept recently. "I guess your brother is investigating her - her death."

"Right. What can I do for you?"

"Give me some idea of what the hell's going on."

I didn't want to tell Finn anything until he'd talked to the police. "What do you already know?"

Finn sighed. "I got the copy of the will, obviously. I called Alex, and she said she'd find out the details. She called back a couple of days later and said she'd talked to the attorney's office and they'd let us know as soon as the estate was settled. Then we got the letters from Gavin Barkley. I talked to Alex a couple of times since then. That's all."

"Did you know she was in LA?"

Finn shook his head slowly. "No. I don't know why she didn't tell me she was coming out here."

"You two were close?"

"Yeah." Finn smiled sadly. "I haven't spoken to my parents for over a year, but Alex and I were still close." He rubbed his face. "God, this is a nightmare."

"When are you meeting with the police?"

"In about an hour." He glanced at his watch. "I don't know how long it will take me to get to the police station."

"From here, at this time of day, about 45 minutes."

He sighed. "I'd better go."

"Do you have a rental?"

"Yeah. It's got GPS. I guess that'll get me there."

I felt bad for anyone unused to driving in LA traffic. "Would you like me to drive you? I'll bring you back to your car."

His expression lightened a bit. "I don't want to inconvenience you."

"I'm happy to do it." I stood. "Come to my office with me while I close up shop."

Finn trailed quietly after me. As we exited the building, I said, "Did you know about the accident, growing up?"

"Yeah. My parents would mention it sometimes, although they tried not to let us overhear. Then I got old enough to realize that my mother never wore a swimsuit or shorts, and I asked her about it. She told me what had happened to her."

"My dad said your mom went through a lot."

"Yeah." Finn sighed. "I don't know if my parents were happily married before the accident because I don't remember. But afterwards it came between them."

"How so?"

"My mother is such a martyr. Everything is always about her. Her last surgery was years and years ago, right? But she still uses her injuries as excuses or as ploys to get people to do things for her. My dad sees through it and won't play along." He grimaced. "They used to have terrible fights. Now they live in separate sections of a big house and barely ever see each other."

"Why did they stay married?"

"My mother liked the perks of being an officer's wife. She'd have lost that if they split up."

"What about your dad?"

Finn shrugged. "He likes having someone to manage the house."

"Jeez. That sounds awful."

"Not a wonderful way to grow up."

"Is your sister close to your parents?"

"No. She was their golden child, growing up, but she finally cut the strings and made her own life."

Finn brightened a bit when he saw the Jeep. "Now this is a vehicle with character."

I laughed. "Yeah, it's a workhorse. It's my fiancé's."

"No kidding. This doesn't look like a woman's ride. I'd like to meet her."

"Ah - it's not a woman's ride. My fiancé is a guy."

"*Seriously.*" Finn brightened even more. "That's one of the many ways in which I've failed to live up to my parents' expectations."

"Being gay?"

"Being gay, going to the University of Georgia instead of the Naval Academy, being a nurse instead of a doctor, moving to liberal

Massachusetts, not appearing on command just because my mother needs a piece of furniture moved and my dad won't do it… The list goes on and on."

"I'm sorry."

"Are you close to your family?"

"Yeah. My dad and brothers have always been supportive. My grandfather helped raise us, and he didn't speak to me for eighteen years. But he finally apologized about a year ago." I glanced at him. "Was Alex supportive of you?"

"Yeah." Finn was looking out the window; I couldn't see his face. "She was."

The visitor parking at the West LA station was full, but I found a spot on the street a couple of blocks away. As we approached the entrance, Finn looked nervous. I said, "Have you had dealings with the police before?"

"No."

"Try not to worry. Kevin and his partner Jon are good at their job. They'll find who did this."

Finn nodded but didn't say anything.

I said hello to the desk sergeant and got our visitor passes. He called back to the detectives' room, and in a minute Kevin appeared. "Finn? I'm Kevin Brodie. Come on back." He jerked his thumb at me and grinned. "Where'd you find him?"

Finn smiled. "I went to UCLA to meet him, and he offered me a ride here."

"Ah." Kevin led us back to the detectives' room. His desk and Jon's were in the near corner; Jon was at his computer and talking on the phone. He spotted us and said, "Gotta go." He stood and held his hand out to Finn. "Mr. Crabtree, I'm Detective Jon Eckhoff. I'm sorry for your loss."

"Thank you. Please call me Finn."

"Sure. Have a seat."

We arranged ourselves around the cubicle. Jon took out his notebook. Kevin said, "When was the last time you spoke to Alex?"

"About two and a half weeks ago, on a Wednesday."

"What did you talk about?"

Finn shrugged. "Work and stuff. Maybe taking a vacation together this summer."

"Did she say anything about coming to Los Angeles?"

"Not a word."

"What did Alex do for a living?"

"She sells - she sold cars for a high-end dealer. Rolls, Bugatti, like that."

"Did she do pretty well with that?"

Finn huffed a laugh. "Oh, hell, yeah. But she was tired of the ass-kissing she had to do with the customers, and the old lechers who kept asking her out. She was going to use the inheritance to quit and move to the Keys."

"Have you or your sister had any contact with any of the other people in the will?"

"I haven't. If Alex did, she didn't tell me about it."

Kevin studied Finn for a moment. "Did you know about the Barkleys before you got the will?"

"Yeah. My parents talked about the accident a good bit."

"Do you know if anyone in your family had been in contact with Gavin?"

"Not that I know of." Finn suddenly made the connection. "Do you think Alex came here to see Gavin? Do you think he killed her?"

"We know she came here to see him. We don't know that he killed her, but they were killed with the same gun." Kevin leaned back, steepling his fingers, resting them on his chin. It was a move he made when he was about to spring something on someone. "When was the last time you spoke to your parents?"

Finn grimaced. "Over a year ago. They've more or less disowned me."

"So you weren't aware that your mother was also in Los Angeles at the time that Gavin Barkley was killed."

Finn gasped. I said, "She came to my house the next morning."

Finn stared at me. "*Why?*"

"I'm not sure. It was an odd visit."

Finn put his hand over his mouth. "Oh my *God*."

Kevin asked, "Do you know if your mother had been checking up on Barkley?"

"I don't know. I do know that she hated him. But -" He closed his eyes, despair on his face. "Oh, God."

"Do you know whether your mother knew how to use a gun?"

Finn gulped. "Not to my knowledge. My dad would go to the range sometimes, but she never went with him. But - I don't know what she's been doing the past couple of years."

"Okay. One more thing. Does the name Jennelle Shifflett mean anything to you?"

Finn shrugged. "I recognize the name from the will, but I'd never heard it before that. Who is she?"

"Good question." Kevin looked at Jon. "Anything else we need right now?"

Jon said, "Can I get your cell phone number, Finn? That way, if we have another question, we can call."

"Sure." Finn gave his number. "When - uh - can I see Alex?"

Kevin said, "Let me call the medical examiner's office. We may be able to go now, if that's okay. You can talk to them about arrangements."

"I left my car in Westwood."

"That's fine. We'll take you back there."

Jon said, "Ah, I did think of one more thing. Do you know if Alex had a will?"

Finn nodded. "She did. She and I had gotten together and made wills and advance directives, all that, so that our parents wouldn't be making decisions for us. We had each other's power of attorney and named each other as next of kin. That's why I'm here and not my mother or father."

Kevin said, "So you know, there was a per stirpes stipulation in Barkley's will. Alex's portion will go to you as her beneficiary."

Finn shook his head, tears in his eyes. "I don't want it. I'd rather they just re-divide it."

Kevin put his hand on Finn's shoulder. "No need to worry about that now."

Jon called the coroner, who said Finn could come now. Jon said, "I'll take him. I live in Westwood anyway. I can drop him at his car."

Finn shook my hand. "Thank you, Jamie."

"Sure. I'm sorry."

He nodded glumly and followed Jon out of the office.

Kevin blew out a breath. "Well. That didn't do anything to ease our suspicions about Marie Crabtree."

"Nope. You going home?"

"Not yet. I'm going to type this up and call Susan."

"Okay. See ya."

Tuesday, April 28

The next morning, Kevin called not long after I got to the office. "You and Liz want to get lunch?"

"Sure. You buying?"

"Of course."

We met at Wilson Plaza. Jon and Kevin brought those delicious tacos, and Liz and I fell on them like starving wolves. I said, "God, these are good. I wish we had food trucks on campus."

Kevin said, "Pfft. You have every kind of food known to man on this campus."

"I know. But these are *good.*"

He laughed. I said, "To what do we owe this visit?"

"We'd been down at Pacific, talking to Susan and Max, and now have to go back to Benedict Canyon to talk to a potential witness who came forward. You guys were on the way."

I said, "Anything new on Susan and Max's end?"

Jon said, "They got a hit on the gun used to kill Barkley. It was the same one used last July in an armed robbery in National City where a shopkeeper was wounded."

I said, "National City? That puts us back in San Diego."

"Yep."

Liz said, "How was Gavin killed with a gun from San Diego?"

Jon wiped his mouth and picked up another taco. "Guns travel. Bad guys pass them around or steal them from each other. But it is an interesting development."

I said, "Have they found Kate Bianchi's brother yet?"

Jon shook his head, his mouth full.

I said, "That could be a San Diego connection, if he still lives there."

Kevin said, "Yes, it could."

We'd finished eating and were still talking when Kristen Beach walked by. She stopped. "Hello, detectives."

Jon grinned. "Ms. Beach. What a lovely surprise."

I said, "Where are you headed?"

"HR. I have to change my direct deposit." She smiled at Kevin. "Did you identify your Jane Doe?"

Kevin smiled back. "We did. Still working on finding her killer, though."

"You'll find him. Or her." She grinned. "See you guys back at the big house. Kevin, Jon, always a pleasure."

Kevin watched her go - but then, so did Jon. Liz smacked him on the arm, but she was laughing. "Cut that out."

Jon grinned at her. "I always save the last dance for you, darlin'." He stood. "We'd better get back in the saddle, cowboy."

I said to Kevin, "Is he like this all the time?"

Kevin rolled his eyes. "You have no idea."

That evening, as I was clearing the table after dinner, Pete went upstairs and returned with a legal pad. "We should do our homework for Dr. Bibbins. Make a list of our long-term goals."

"Okay." I'd kept her instructions in the back of my mind but hadn't written anything down. "The first thing I think we should do is make arrangements to take care of our dads."

"Agreed." Pete wrote that down. "Jeff and Kevin will join you in that, won't they?"

"Yes. We'll set up something separate for your dad."

"Okay." Pete made a couple of notes. "What else?"

I leaned back in my chair, rubbing my hands through my hair. "How long do you want to work?"

"I - don't know." Pete tapped the pen against his chin. "I've assumed for so long that I'd be working until at least 67, if not longer - it's hard to imagine stopping before that without a plan for what I'd do instead." He gave me a close look. "I thought you said you didn't want to quit your job."

"I don't. But I do want to spend more time with our distant families now. We couldn't afford to buy plane tickets before; now we can. If one or both of us is still working a Monday to Friday job, we'll be tied to traveling on the weekends. I've used a lot of vacation over the past year, and I won't have a lot left after our honeymoon."

Pete mused for a minute. "We've agreed, we're not going to change our employment status for at least a year, right?"

"Right."

"So, for the next year, let's try the weekend travel thing. We do need to spend more time with our families. Mine is all mostly in one place now, so that's convenient."

"My grandfather is ninety. He's healthy, but he's ninety. But - we can't be gone every weekend."

"No. And once we start construction on our house, we'll have to spend some time in Alamogordo, too."

"How about once a month, for now? We'll alternate between Tucson and Jacksonville. The house construction won't begin for a year, and we should be able to handle everything with the architect online until then."

"Okay." Pete made another note. "That's a short-term solution to a long-term goal."

I chuckled. "Yeah, well, one step at a time."

Pete frowned. "I won't have as much time to cook."

"It'll only be one weekend a month. We've got that freezer now; we'll eat out of the freezer the week after we go out of town."

He nodded. "I'd better get it filled up while I'm off this summer in that case."

"All right, that's two long-term goals. Take care of our dads and travel to see our families more."

"And the new house counts as a long-term goal."

I said, "It certainly does."

"I did some calculations." Pete pulled a folded sheet of paper from the back of the legal pad. "I assume we want Lauren to invest the money to avoid taxes as much as possible, right?"

"Right."

"How do you feel about the stock market?"

"I don't understand it."

"No one does." Pete grinned. "I had a conversation with one of our business instructors today. He said you might as well play the slots."

"Interest rates are so low, though…"

"True. But Jerry said you shouldn't put anything into the market that you're not prepared to lose. Because there is a chance that you could lose it all. He thinks the bubble is going to burst within the next few years." He tapped the piece of paper he'd unfolded. "The average of those CD rates at the credit union is one percent. One percent of $38 million is $380,000 a year. Even if we spent $18 million on various things, we'd have an income of $200,000 a year without ever touching the principal."

"I don't know if I can spend $18 million."

"I know. So say we have a principal of $25 million. Even if it made no interest at all, if you withdrew $500,000 to live on every year, it would last you fifty years. Withdraw $250,000, it'll last a hundred years. *We* won't last a hundred years."

I blew out a breath. "We have to decide whether we want to spend it down or not. If not, who are we going to leave it to? My nephews won't need it. They'll have what's left of Jeff's share."

Pete nodded. "I'd like to help pay for my nieces' education so they can start adulthood without student loan debt. But I don't know that I'd want to leave a pile of money to them. If they knew it was coming, they might make different choices in their lives. I want them to be independent."

I tapped Pete's legal pad. "Write that down. Help pay for Steph and Sam's college and grad school."

"That's okay with you?"

"Of course it's okay with me. They're my nieces, too."

Pete grinned. "Thank you."

I gave him a "you should know that" look. "If we're not going to leave it to people, we should leave it to worthy causes. I want to use part of it, once we start using it, to establish a scholarship fund at UCLA for children of combat veterans."

"Oh, that's an excellent idea. How much would that take?"

"I don't know. I'm pretty sure Kevin would want to join in on that, so half would come from each of us. I do know that we'd turn the money over to the UCLA Foundation, and they'd manage it."

Pete said, "We could leave what's left to UCLA in our wills. Add to the scholarships or leave it to the libraries." He made another note. "So can we say that one of our long-term goals is to stay out of the stock market?"

"Yes. I don't want any of this money lining the pockets of any Wall Street types or CEOs. If that means we have to give more of it away to nonprofits, so be it."

"Agreed." Pete clicked his pen open and closed a couple of times. "While we're talking about goals - do you want to talk about our wedding vows?"

"Um - can we do that some other time? It's getting late. One major topic at a time is enough for me."

Pete laid his pen down and inclined his head to me. "As you wish."

I laughed. "Thanks, Westley."

Wednesday, April 29

First thing Wednesday morning, I got a call from Michelle Richardson at Gordon Smith's office. "Your money will be released on Thursday, so it should be in your account by Tuesday. I need your account number."

"Okay." I recited the number to her from memory. "Thanks, Michelle."

"You're welcome. Next time you're in San Diego you can buy me a drink. Or two."

I was walking back to my office after leaving the reference desk when I got a text from Kevin. He'd included Pete on it as well. *You guys going to be home tonight?*

Pete answered back more quickly than I could. He was already home. *Yeah. Want to come over?*

Yes. Have something to talk about.

OK. Dinnertime or later?

Dinnertime.

OK we'll feed you.

I finally got a word in. *See you then.* I wondered what was up.

I turned onto 17th Street just as Kevin drove past me. I saw him park a couple of blocks beyond our building, and we reached our front gate at the same time. I pushed the gate open. "What's up?"

Kevin shook his head. "Later."

He looked tired. I opened the front door and called, "Hi, honey, we're home."

Pete looked down from the kitchen. "Hey, good timing. The grill's hot."

We grilled fish and ate on the back deck. Kevin wasn't saying much. We talked about the Dodgers and Padres while we ate.

Afterward, I carried our plates in and returned with a beer for each of us. Pete lifted his. "To baseball."

Kevin and I both chimed in, and Kevin's face relaxed a little. We all drank.

Pete said, "Okay, Kev. What's going on?"

Kevin looked down at his bottle then up at us. "Abby broke up with me last night."

Pete sucked in a breath. I said, "Wow. That's - for good?"

"I guess. She's staying at Amy's right now."

Pete found his voice. "This is not only about the money."

Kevin sighed. "No, it just gave her an excuse."

I thought back to the time when Abby lived with Kevin and me. She had done some complaining about his irregular hours - but otherwise, they'd seemed solid. "It's hard to believe."

"I know."

I remembered Abby telling us about the house she and Kevin had eventually bought together. "She was so excited about the house and the workshop."

"I know. I told her she could keep the house. I'll pay off the mortgage then sign a quitclaim deed."

I said, "Oh, *Kev*."

He shook his head. "This is the second time I'm having to climb out of a financial hole that a woman put me in. At least this time I can afford it."

Pete said, "Did you tell her you knew about Sean?"

"Yep." Kevin picked at the label of his beer bottle. "She was furious. Cussed Liz up and down for telling."

I said, "She didn't tell Liz to not talk to Pete."

"I told her that. Pissed her off even more."

Pete said, "Maybe she's trying to protect you and the inheritance from Sean, if he's back sniffing around."

Kevin barked a laugh. "I don't think so."

We sat in silence for a minute. I said, "What are you going to do?"

"I'm gonna move my stuff this weekend. Next week when the money clears, I'll take care of the house. The mortgage is with the credit union, so it shouldn't be a problem." He finished his beer and rubbed his face. "I want to move back to Westwood. I'm thinking I'll buy a condo, maybe near Jon and Liz."

I said, "Can Abby afford the property taxes and everything on her own?"

Kevin shrugged. "Won't be my problem, will it?"

"I guess not."

Pete said, "Another beer?"

"Yeah."

He went inside and returned with three more bottles. "Do you want to stay here tonight?"

Kevin looked a bit less glum. "Do you mind? I brought my clothes and stuff this time."

I said, "Of course we don't mind."

"Thanks." He smiled wanly. "I owe you guys."

"Nah. Have you told Dad?"

"No." Kevin sighed.

Pete said, "Do you want to stay here until you find a place?"

I shot Pete a grateful look. It would be a bit crowded, but Kevin had taken me in after Ethan had split up with me. I could do no less for him.

Kevin looked unsure - an unusual expression for him. "I don't want to invade your privacy."

I waved a hand in dismissal. "Don't worry about that. It won't be for long."

"No. As soon as the money settles, I'll find a place and be out of your hair." Kevin sighed deeply. "I really appreciate this, guys. I'll pay rent."

Pete waved that off. "Don't bother. You're not going to be here long enough for that."

"You're sure?"

"Yep."

I said, "Do you want us to come on Saturday and help you move out?"

"That'd be great." Kevin's phone rang and he looked at the screen. "It's Susan." He stood to go inside.

We trailed in after him. I started washing up; Pete went upstairs to fix the sofa bed. Kevin said, "Hey, Susan. No, I'm at Jamie's. What's up?" He listened for a minute. "Phoenix? You confirmed it? So much for that angle. Oh, what?" He made a face of surprise and looked at me. "No shit. That's excellent. Tell Max he's ready for D-II. Yeah, I'll tell them. Thanks, Susan."

Pete had come back downstairs. "Tell us what?"

"Susan and Max found Vince Bianchi. San Diego PD brought him in, and they went down today to talk to him. He's an upstanding citizen. Says he's always thought Gavin Barkley was a stupid kid who made a terrible mistake. It ruined his parents' and sister's lives but he wouldn't let it ruin his. And he has an alibi that checks out. He was at a sales convention in Phoenix that entire weekend."

I asked, "So why is Max ready for D-II?"

"He got inspired. When Bianchi said he was in Phoenix, it occurred to Max that if Jennelle Shifflett wasn't in California, she might be nearby. They searched in Arizona and Nevada and found her. She lives in a trailer park on the outskirts of Vegas. They've called Vegas PD to bring her in tomorrow, and they're going to talk to her."

I said, "Hey, good for Max."

Pete said, "They never got Gordon Smith to tell them anything?"

"No. They were working on a subpoena, but it hadn't come through yet. Now they won't need it."

Thursday, April 30

At work the next morning, I told Liz about Kevin and Abby. She shook her head. "I feel bad for Kevin, but I'm not surprised at all."

"When you were having drinks with her that night, did she say anything about her older sister?"

"Yeah. She said she'd been going to the sister for advice."

"I figured." I gave Liz a pointed look. "You'd better make sure your path doesn't cross Abby's. Kevin said she tore you a new one."

Liz shrugged. "She shouldn't have been so specific. If she'd said, 'Don't tell anyone,' I wouldn't have."

"Not even Jon?"

Liz considered that. "I would have told him sooner or later. I see how you and Pete operate - you tell each other everything. My parents are the same way, and they've been married for thirty-four years. I think that's the way to be, isn't it?"

"It works for us. I don't know if it works for everyone."

"Kevin would have found out somehow. At least he'd have noticed the withdrawals from their account. Stuff like that never stays hidden."

"Kevin's going to buy a condo somewhere in Westwood. He said maybe near you guys."

Liz looked concerned. "Is he going to quit the force?"

"No. At least not yet. Was Jon worried that he might?"

"We'd wondered about it. Kevin's good for Jon, you know. He says he enjoys work now more than he ever has." She bit her lip. "You're not going to quit, are you?"

"Nope." I grinned. "I don't want to go through the hassle of having to buy my own health insurance."

"Ha!" Liz grinned then sobered. "You know, in two-plus years of being a cop's girlfriend, I've learned something I don't think Abby ever did."

"What's that?"

"The bond between partners. Especially partners who get along. It's like a marriage itself. You can't be jealous of it."

"You are a wise woman, Ms. Nguyen."

She poked me in the chest. "We're partners too. If you're gonna bug out on me, you'd better give me plenty of warning."

"Oh, believe me. You'll be the second to know."

Kevin got home about a half hour after I did, carrying a full gym bag. "Just enough clothes to get me to the weekend."

Pete said, "After dinner, we'd better move some things around in the storage unit for your boxes and stuff."

"Okay." Kevin dropped his bag on the landing and peered into the pot of simmering pasta sauce. "Good God, do you guys eat like this all the time?"

I grinned. "Why do you think we work out so much?"

"Yeah, I'd better get in on that."

"Are you still swimming?"

"I haven't been. That's another reason to move to Westwood. I can use the North Pool in the mornings."

When we got seated for dinner, I said, "Anything to report? Did Susan and Max talk to Jennelle Shifflett?"

"They did. She's a dealer at one of the casinos, in her mid-thirties. She met old man Barkley at the casino when she was twenty-two, before his wife died. She said he treated her well. She got a regular stipend from him in return for having sex with him whenever he came to town."

Pete raised his eyebrows. "I guess that's legal in Nevada."

I said, "A monogamous hooker?"

"More or less. Anyway, she never met Gavin, had no reason to want him dead. She hadn't looked up any of the other heirs; she figured $38 million was enough. She was working both nights when Alex and Gavin were killed, and Susan and Max confirmed that with her boss."

I frowned. "Another dead end."

"Yeah. But Jon and I had a very interesting conversation today. With Marie Crabtree."

Pete said, "Oh?"

"We called her mostly to ask her about her daughter, right? But she didn't realize that; she started talking about Gavin."

I said, "No. She did *not* admit to killing him."

Kevin gave me a "don't be stupid" look. "Of course not. But she's afraid she's responsible for his death."

"Why?"

"The day Gavin got out of jail and called all the parents? Marie freaked out, same as Belinda. She called Belinda as soon as she got off the phone. Marie said she told Belinda, 'Hasn't he caused us enough pain? Why can't he just disappear and leave us alone?' I told her, Brian has an alibi and Belinda obviously couldn't have done it - who is she suspicious of? She doesn't know. But she's afraid she set something in motion."

Pete said, "Like what?"

"She didn't know. But it's an interesting thought, isn't it?" Kevin sprinkled some more cheese on his spaghetti.

I said, "Why was Marie in LA?"

"She told us that Alex came to LA to help Gavin in response to the letter Gavin wrote. She wanted to give him money to help him get on his feet. Marie followed Alex here to talk her out of seeing Gavin. But when she got here, Alex wasn't answering her phone, and Marie panicked. She was afraid Gavin had harmed Alex in retaliation for his jail sentence."

Pete said, "That explains why she was so nervous when she came here."

I said, "But why would Gavin kill Alex? She might have been willing to keep helping him. An alliance with her may have been a way for Gavin to get some of his father's money back, but that wouldn't work if she was dead."

Pete said, "Besides, Gavin was a drunk driver. From what everyone else has said, he didn't strike me as the recidivist type."

"No." Kevin pointed his fork in the general direction of the ocean. "Max did some leg work in the bars along the boardwalk in Venice, and a couple of bartenders remembered Gavin. The reason that they remembered was that he drank soda rather than alcohol. He didn't even have a beer."

I said, "Sure would be nice if you could trace that gun."

Kevin snorted. "Nice doesn't begin to cover it."

I took advantage of my reference shift on Friday to look for land in Alamogordo. Lots in developments there were inexpensive, but I wasn't sure we wanted to be in a development. I found several that looked like good candidates and emailed the links to Pete.

I beat Kevin home. Pete was cooking tonight - we'd put Date Night on hold while Kevin was staying with us. I went up to the kitchen and kissed Pete. "Did you get my email?"

"Yeah. Go grab the laptop, and we'll look at them while we're waiting for Kev."

I quickly changed clothes and brought Pete's laptop to the kitchen. He opened his email, and we began examining the lots. By the time Kevin got home, an hour had passed, and we had a short list of three. Pete said, "I'll email these to Steve and have him check them out over the weekend."

I said, "Do you have a favorite?"

"Yeah." He grinned at me. "Do you?"

"Uh huh. Which is yours?"

"Which is *yours?*"

"No way. I asked first."

He laughed. "The most expensive one."

"Good. Mine too." The lot was in town, within walking distance of Steve, but backed up to federal land. It was the biggest of those we'd looked at and had no homeowners' association restrictions. "Have Steve ask if geothermal is possible on the sites."

"I will."

Kevin said, "Geothermal? For heat?"

"And a/c. Fuel-free, not even dependent on sunlight. Completely sustainable and off the grid."

"I thought you were going solar."

"Oh, we will for everything else. For heat and cooling, though, geothermal's the way. And New Mexico is perfect for it."

"Is it expensive?"

"It's expensive to install, but after that it's cheap and clean. And it's not like we can't afford it."

He grinned. "True."

As we ate, Kevin updated us on the case. It was getting to be a habit. He said, "We sent Max and Jon to San Diego today to talk to the guys who'd investigated that armed robbery last summer. They had a guy they'd liked for it but could never get enough evidence."

"Who?"

"His name is Orlando Howell. A couple of the people in the store thought they recognized him, even though he was wearing a mask. He's a known felon, been in and out of jail since juvie."

"Did they question him at the time?"

"Sure. His brother gave him an alibi but no one else could confirm it. They were pretty sure he was their guy, but they weren't able to pin it on him. They were *intensely* interested to learn that the gun had been used to kill two people in LA."

Pete said, "I bet."

"San Diego PD is gonna put out a BOLO on him. If they find him, Susan and Max will go back down and talk to him."

Saturday, May 2

The next morning, we drove to Brentwood to borrow one of Ali's trucks and pick up Mel who was going to help us move Kevin's stuff. We stopped at Liz and Jon's next so they could join the caravan. When we got to Glendale, Kevin unlocked the door. The house was dim, shades pulled down and quiet. So quiet. Kevin stood in the middle of the living room and took a deep breath, then blew it out. "Okay. All the furniture stays, except for my office chair. From the kitchen I'm going to take what was mine before Abby and I got together. Jamie, you can help me there, 'cause you'll recognize those things. Pete and Mel, you can get my clothes and stuff from the bedroom."

"Roger that."

We worked all morning, boxing up dishes and utensils, books and clothes, pictures and mementoes. Kevin dragged his safe from the office closet into the living room. The computer in the office was his; Liz dismantled that and carried the components into the living room.

Jon came out of the bedroom carrying a baseball bat and the knee brace that Kevin had worn after his arthroscopy more than a year ago now. "You want these, right?"

"Yeah. That brace was expensive."

We worked all morning and had the truck, Jeep, and Kevin's car loaded by early afternoon. Kevin texted Abby to let her know we were finished. She responded promptly. I said, "What did she say?"

"Thank you."

"That's it?"

"Yep."

Ending not with a bang but a whimper. We locked the house and went to the vehicles. Mel said, "Ali will be home by the time we get back. Why don't you all stop, and we'll have lunch at the house? Then Ali will help us unload."

We agreed and set off for Brentwood. When we got to Ali and Mel's, Ali had just gotten home with Thai food for everyone. We washed up and went out on the back patio to eat.

Ali and Mel had held a quick conference in their kitchen. While Ali distributed the food, Mel said, "Kev, you should stay with us until you get a place. We have a lot more room."

Ali said, "You'd have your own suite at the other end of the house from ours. There's a fridge in the wet bar, and plenty of room for all your things. You'd have a bedroom and an office, already furnished. We've got extra keys too."

Mel added, "And we have a pool."

Kevin said, "Oh, wow. I don't know. That's awfully generous."

Mel dismissed that. "What's generous? We have all this space that almost never gets used. And it'll be easier to coordinate the law firm work."

Ali said, "You guys will be falling over each other at Pete and Jamie's. You've got plenty of room to spread out here. And parking isn't a problem like it is in Santa Monica."

Kevin looked at me. "What do you think?"

I said, "I think it sounds great. Not that we wouldn't love to have you, and it would work out fine, but there are definite advantages for you being here."

Kevin thought for a minute then smiled at Mel. "Okay. Thank you. I owe you guys."

"Pfft." Ali smacked him on the shoulder. "What are friends for?"

After we ate, we unloaded all of Kevin's stuff. The guest suite was perfect, two large rooms set up as a bedroom and an office, with plenty of empty drawers and shelving and an enormous walk-in closet. The bathroom was luxurious, with a shower *and* a whirlpool tub, and Kevin had his own French doors that opened onto the back patio and the pool area. He'd be able to slip out and swim early in the morning or late at night without bothering Ali or Mel. The

TV/family/game room was just down the hall, with a wet bar and fridge.

I personally thought Kevin might never want to leave.

We stacked the boxes of dishes and things he wouldn't need for a while in the closet. When we were finished, we all had a beer on the back porch. We were talking about the best condo buildings in Westwood when Kevin's phone rang.

He answered, "Hey, Susan, what's up? No shit. Jon and Jamie are here. Can I put you on speaker?"

He hit the speaker button and set his phone on the table; we all huddled around it. Susan's voice said, "Orlando Howell? Our person of interest? Turned up in the ER with a knife wound to the chest."

Jon said, "Excellent. Did he say who did it?"

"Yeah, he blamed his brother. Said they had an argument about a debt."

Kevin said, "Is this the same brother who alibied him for the robbery?"

"The very one. So now we're looking for him. If they've had a falling out, he may be willing to drop that alibi story in exchange for reduced charges on the stabbing."

I said, "We still don't know if he had any connection to Gavin Barkley or Alex Crabtree, though."

"No, but if we can tie him to that robbery, that ties him to the gun. Then he's got some 'splainin' to do."

Kevin said, "That's great, Susan. Let us know."

We left Kevin at Ali and Mel's and drove home. My shoulder was aching after all the packing and carrying; Pete saw me carefully stretching it. "Want a rubdown?"

"Absolutely."

We took a quick shower to warm my muscles, then Pete put me through my stretching exercises and gave me a good massage. Afterwards, we put on t-shirts and shorts, cued up some music and cuddled on the living room sofa. I said, "I need to take the sheets off the sofa bed and wash them."

"Do that tomorrow, why don'tcha?"

"Yeah, it can wait."

Pete grinned. "Is Mr. Clean relaxing his standards?"

"Don't get your hopes up. I just don't want to use my shoulder any more this evening."

He chuckled into my hair. "Let's talk about our new house."

"Okay. Was Steve going to call you about the lot tonight?"

"Tomorrow. He was only able to see one of them today, so he said he'd email tomorrow after he'd seen them all."

"Okay, good. We should look at floor plans."

"Yeah, but I don't want to get the computer out now. Let's just talk about basics. How much space do we need?"

I thought for a moment. "Enough for our families. But not too big. And no sharing bathrooms." I'd done enough of that as a kid.

Pete made a note. "Bathrooms for everyone. Do you want a swimming pool?"

"No. They're too much trouble to maintain. We'll just go to the Y in Alamogordo. They have one, don't they?"

"I'm not sure. We'll find out. Obviously we need a kitchen."

"Obviously. You get to design that. Do you want a living and dining room?"

"No. Too formal. I want an eat-in kitchen, but big enough for more than two of us, and a great room. Family room. Whatever you want to call it."

"I agree. Oh, back to the bathrooms. We should put in tankless water heaters for the showers, like the ones we saw in England. Then we don't have to install a huge water heater that eats up power."

"Good idea. Showers or bathtubs?"

"Hm. One bathtub. I don't know which bathroom it should be in, though. Not ours."

"We'll think about that." Pete made more notes. "I want a big pantry attached to the kitchen."

"Of course. What about the master suite?"

"The one at Ali and Mel's, where Kevin's staying, is just about perfect, with the office and bedroom forming a suite."

"With the bathroom in between. And a big walk-in closet somewhere."

"Yes. Built-ins all around the closet and office."

"Yeah. I guess Abby won't be doing built-ins for us anymore."

"I know." Pete sighed. "Think they're done for good?"

I considered that. "Yeah. I do. I think Abby will regret it, probably sooner rather than later, but Kevin won't look back."

"No. He won't."

We were quiet for a minute then Pete said, "Back to the house. Ali can do the desert xeriscaping for us, right?"

"Sure. We'll have to see if we can grow anything besides cacti."

"I know the prickly pear cactus has edible parts. We'll have some of those."

"I'll do some research on that. We need rain barrels on all our gutter downspouts."

"Yes." Pete made a note. "We may have to have a custom blueprint done."

"Maybe. I don't know any architects."

"I'm sure that someone we know does."

I wiggled back against Pete. "Now I'm anxious to get started on this."

"We need to take our time, though. Get it right the first time. And remember, Lauren said to buy the land but not to start building yet."

"I know. That doesn't mean we can't be ready to build when the time comes."

Pete began playing with my hair, wrapping curls around his fingers. "We may like the house so much we decide to move there."

I pulled back and looked at him. "Would you want to live there full-time?"

"I don't know. Probably not. You'd have to drive to Las Cruces, to New Mexico State, for a university job."

"If they even had an opening."

"We could teach online."

"How about if that's our fallback plan, for if and when we're tired of the Monday-Friday gig."

I felt him smile against the back of my head. "I like it."

Sunday, May 3

We spent the next morning doing chores. At midday, we went to Neil and Mark's to do some wedding planning. They were hosting our reception, and we had decisions to make.

Our wedding itself was going to be immediate family only - my dad, our siblings, nieces and nephews. Neil was getting his "deputy for a day" certificate and would perform the ceremony; Ali and Mel would be there. Everyone else - friends, coworkers and more distant family - was invited to the reception. We figured around fifty people, if everyone showed up. Which they'd all promised to do.

Neil wanted to talk about food. He, Mark, Ali and Mel were all chipping in to pay for the reception as their gift to us. I couldn't think of a better present. When we pulled up in the circular driveway, Mel's car was already there.

Neil came to the door and ushered us in. "Go on through. Grab a drink on your way. I've got to make a quick call."

We went through the house and got drinks from the fridge. An enormous glassed-in porch stretched across the entire back of the house, opening onto an equally large space that was deck at one end and a covered outdoor kitchen at the other. It was perfect for entertaining a crowd.

Ali, Mel and Mark were sprawled on deck chairs; Ali lifted a glass to me. I said, "No, no, please don't get up."

They laughed. Pete said, "How's your boarder settling in?"

"He hasn't had much chance yet." Mel made a face. "He left us a note this morning, said he had to go to San Diego to question a suspect."

I said, "Oho. I hope that's good news."

Neil came out to join us, rubbing his hands together. "All right, guys. What do you want to eat at your reception?"

Pete and I looked at each other and shrugged; we hadn't discussed this at all. I said, "Something that fits the lumberjack theme."

"*Lumberjack?*"

I explained. Ali said, "Oh my God, you're having a *lesbian* wedding."

We hooted with laughter. Once we'd settled down Neil said, "As entertaining as that is, I refuse to serve rabbit stew and baked beans at your reception."

We riffed on the idea of rabbit stew for a minute before Pete snapped his fingers. "I know the perfect meal. Easy to fix, no catering required, and beloved by all the Brodies. And me."

I had no idea what he was talking about. Neil said, "What?"

"A Lowcountry boil. We had one at Jamie's uncle's house last spring."

Neil's confusion cleared. "Ah, yes. I've attended a couple of those at Dave's over the years."

Ali said, "So have we. And it's beloved by me too."

Mark had grown up in Seattle and was looking at us all like we were nuts. "What the hell is a Lowcountry boil?"

I explained. "Shrimp, Andouille sausage, corn on the cob, red potatoes, and spices. Boiled all together and dumped out on a picnic table to eat. Everyone in my family knows how to do it, but my Aunt Linda's recipe is the best."

Neil rubbed his hands together. "Excellent. I'll get in touch with Linda. What about a cake?"

We decided on a sheet cake rather than a layered monstrosity - carrot cake, Pete's favorite and one I liked just fine. Neil made notes, then checked his list. "Okay. I think that's everything. Now, have you talked about vows?"

We looked at each other again. Pete said, "Uh - no."

"Okay, there's no rush on that. But don't forget."

We hung out talking for a while longer. When we got ready to go, Mel said, "Tuesday's the big day, right?"

I said, "Big day?"

She gave me a "duh" look. "That's when the money hits your account."

"Oh. Right." In spite of our talk about building a house, I'd almost forgotten about the money.

Ali laughed. "You're taking Lauren's advice to heart. Not only are you not acting rich, you don't even remember that you're rich."

"It still doesn't seem real to me."

Mel said, "It may never seem real to you."

When we got home, Pete went to the kitchen to put together our lunches for tomorrow. I said, "Do you think Steve has seen our lot yet?"

Pete chuckled. "*Our* lot?"

"Okay, our potential lot."

"He should have. Check to see if he's emailed us."

I brought the laptop downstairs and logged on. "Yeah, here's a message from him. He says, 'Hi guys, your favorite lot is definitely the best one. Best location, least amount of work to get the lot ready, etc. etc. You need to come see it soon - it might not last long.'"

Pete grinned. "We can fly out there this weekend."

"Yep." I opened a new tab to look for flights. "And we can fly first class."

I'd booked our flight and had taken the laptop back upstairs when the doorbell rang. I heard Pete say, "Hey," then heard Kevin's voice.

I trotted downstairs. "Hey, Mel and Ali said you went to San Diego."

"Yep." He tossed his jacket on the loveseat and sat beside it. "Susan and I went down this morning to talk to these brothers."

"And?"

Kevin smiled tiredly. "We got 'em."

"Them?"

"Yeah." He propped his feet up on the ottoman. "Orlando Howell said his brother stabbed him over a debt, right? San Diego PD picked up the brother in the wee hours this morning. Javier Howell. Orlando has a long sheet, but Javier had no adult record. He's skirted around the law some but had avoided arrest until now. He told us everything."

Pete said, "Hoping to get a deal?"

"Yeah. And he may get one. Not up to me. Anyway, it was a paid hit. Javier says he met with a guy who gave him thirty grand in cash, fifteen up front and fifteen after Orlando killed Gavin."

Pete said, "A *paid* hit?"

"Yep. Neither Orlando nor Javier had any connection to the Barkleys beforehand. Javier says he was approached by the guy a week before the murder. The guy had a news clipping with an old picture of Gavin and told Javier that Gavin was getting out of jail on Wednesday and headed for Los Angeles. Orlando used to live in LA, so he knew his way around."

I said, "What about Alex Crabtree?"

Kevin shook his head. "Wrong place, wrong time. Orlando tracked Gavin to his motel room and knocked on the door. Gavin was in the bathroom; Alex opened the door and Orlando fired. Gavin climbed out the back window, but Orlando couldn't give chase because he had to deal with Alex's body. He put her in his car, threw her phone and purse off the end of the pier, drove to Benedict Canyon and dumped her, then went back to Venice. He drove her rental to the airport and left it in the lot with the keys in it, then took the shuttle back to Venice. He started looking around for Gavin and finally tracked him down the next evening."

Pete said, "Who paid them?"

"Don't know." Kevin sighed. "All Javier could say was that it was an adult white male of average height without a distinguishing voice or accent of any kind. The guy wore a ski mask and gloves at their meetings."

Pete asked, "How did he choose Javier?"

"The guy wouldn't say."

I said, "Javier met with the money man in San Diego?"

"Yeah."

"So San Diego is going to keep looking for the guy who ordered the hit?"

"Of course, but they have absolutely nothing to go on." Kevin yawned. "Susan, Max, Jon and I got our shooter. That'll have to do for now."

Pete said, "Why wouldn't this man approach Orlando himself?"

Kevin shrugged. "Beats me. We questioned Javier extensively about the money man, and I'm confident that he was telling us everything he knew."

I asked, "Is there any way to trace the money?"

Kevin snorted. "Nope. They'd spent at least half of it already. San Diego found the rest at Orlando's apartment, but it was small bills that had been in circulation for a while. It didn't come fresh from the bank."

Pete frowned. "Who's in San Diego? Who knew that Gavin was coming to LA? Who could afford to pay thirty grand for a hit?"

Kevin and I looked at each other. I said, "Gordon Smith."

Pete said, "If it was him, they'll never pin it on him."

I said, "He wouldn't have done it himself. He'd have enlisted several layers of minions."

Kevin said, "True. I'll inform San Diego about that theory. Maybe they can do something with it."

I said, "Did you call Marie Crabtree?"

"I did. Jon called Finn."

"How did Marie react?"

Kevin shook his head. "She's wrecked."

We sat in silence for a minute. Pete said, "One decision. One night in 1980, Gavin chooses not to call a cab. The consequences keep rolling on through the decades."

I said, "Speaking of consequences - we get the money Tuesday."

"I know." Kevin rubbed his face. "I'm going to take that afternoon off, go to the credit union and pay off the mortgage for Abby."

"Then you can start looking for a condo."

"Yeah. One thing at a time." He stood. "Okay, I'll see you guys later. I've got to go unpack."

Pete said, "Good work, detective."

A wry smile. "Yeah, thanks."

We saw Kevin out. Pete climbed the stairs to the kitchen. "Want a beer?"

"Please. Mind if I turn on the news?"

"No, go ahead."

I chose one of the local network affiliates. Pete sat beside me and handed over my beer just as the announcer said, "Two men were arrested today in San Diego for a pair of murders in Los Angeles last month. Brothers Javier and Orlando Howell are being held without bond for the shooting deaths of Alexandra Crabtree, of Coral Gables, Florida, and Gavin Barkley, of Los Angeles. Orlando Howell has been charged with first-degree murder, and Javier Howell has been charged with accessory to murder."

The Howell brothers' mug shots flashed onto the screen - and I whispered, "Oh, *fuck*."

Pete looked at me in surprise. "What?"

Should I tell Pete? I had to.

"I know who paid the Howells." I told him how I knew.

Pete was silent for a minute. The newscaster switched to the next story. Pete said, "Are you sure?"

"Yes."

"Eyewitness accounts are notoriously inaccurate. Are you *positive?*"

I knew what I'd seen. "Yes."

A commercial came on and Pete clicked the mute button. "What are you going to do?"

I picked up my phone. "I'm going to take a personal day tomorrow."

Part 3

Dearly beloved, avenge not yourselves ... for it is written, Vengeance is *mine*; I will repay, saith the Lord. - Romans 12:19, KJV

Monday, May 4

First thing in the morning, I had my final appointment with the orthopedic surgeon. He declared my shoulder healed and gave me permission to begin swimming - although I had to wait another six weeks to resume rugby. As I left the medical office building, I called my dad to tell him I was coming to town.

I got to El Camino Assisted Living around eleven, like I had before, figuring that Belinda's morning routine would be done by then. When I rang the doorbell, a young African-American woman wearing a scrub suit with a floral top answered the door. "Yes?"

"Hi, my name is Jamie Brodie. I'm a friend of the Marcuses. Is this a good time to talk to Belinda for a few minutes?"

The girl frowned. "I'll have to check."

"Of course."

She went to the patio, where I'd sat with Brian and Belinda during my first visit. She disappeared off to the side, then returned to the door and opened it. "Mrs. Marcus says come on in."

I said, "I'm not messing up your routine, am I?"

"No, I've gotta strip the bed and do laundry." She smiled at me. "But thanks for asking. You're the only one that ever has."

I smiled back. "Hey, I'm a working guy too."

Her smile broadened into a grin. "You know where to find her?"

"Yes, ma'am. Thanks."

"She has any trouble, holler for me." The girl headed off down the hallway to the left.

The French doors to the patio were open. Belinda was off to the right, smelling a gorgeous pink rose that hung from its bush at just the right height. She turned her chair and smiled, but her eyes were serious. "Hello, Jamie."

"Hi, Belinda. I hope this isn't a bad time."

"No, not at all." She lifted her shoulder, and I took her hand. "It's always good to see you. Please, have a seat. Tea?"

There was a pitcher of iced tea on a tray with several glasses, sitting on a side table. One glass was already poured, with a straw sticking in it. I poured myself a glass. "Would you like a drink of yours?"

"Please."

I held the glass and guided the straw to Belinda's lips, and she drank. "Thank you." She looked at me solemnly. "You're a kind young man."

I set her glass on the table and picked up my own. "I was raised right."

"Yes, you were."

"Is Brian home?"

"No. He volunteers at a shelter downtown on Mondays." She smiled, but there was a touch of grimness about it. "He says it makes him feel better about our situation, to help so many who are worse off than we are."

I sat my glass back on the table. Even though I'd drunk some, my mouth was still dry. "It's been difficult for him."

"Yes." She gazed at me steadily. "It's been difficult for all of us."

"Of course."

"But you're right, Brian has suffered too. He had to retire much earlier than he had planned to take care of me."

I took another drink of tea. Might as well get to it. "You have a new caretaker?"

Belinda's expression was guarded. "Yes. Tameka. She's a lovely girl. I think she'll work out."

"What happened to Francesca?"

Belinda didn't blink. "She resigned."

"It must be difficult, breaking in a new caretaker."

"I've had so many caretakers over the years. One gets used to it, in a way."

"I suppose you would." I took one more drink of tea and set the glass down again, then pulled my chair closer to Belinda's and lowered my voice. "The day I was here before, I left at the same time as Francesca."

Belinda's expression flattened. "My caretakers only work half-days on Saturday."

"Her ride arrived as I was talking to Brian in the driveway. Her boyfriend, I'm guessing. I got a good look at his face."

"Did you?"

"I did. Imagine my surprise when I saw Javier Howell's mug shot on the news."

Belinda searched my face for a minute. I didn't say anything. Pete had told me once that when questioning someone, if you kept quiet for a while, the suspect would usually say something to relieve the tense silence.

Belinda didn't disappoint. She finally said, "There's no proof."

"I'm sure there's not. How long had you been planning this?"

"Thirty years." Belinda raised her chin. "It gave me purpose."

Maybe *that* was why she'd snapped out of the depression Brian had mentioned. "You saved up the cash bit by bit?"

"I told Brian I needed it for tipping my caretakers. I only used half for that."

Thirty grand in thirty years? I said, "Brian didn't help?"

Finally, her expression changed - it grew fierce. She hissed, "He knew *nothing*. I would *never* involve him." She glared at me.

I said, "Josh wasn't your middleman?"

Belinda turned pale but remained defiant. "*No*. My family has been through enough. I would *never* endanger any of them in that way."

I didn't believe her. "I suppose you won't tell me who your accomplice was."

"You suppose correctly. It. Was. Not. Josh."

For what that was worth. "Marie told the police that she was afraid she'd set something in motion. But she didn't, did she? It was already in motion."

"*Gavin Barkley* set this in motion. I did this for Marie. For Tracy and Julie. For *all* of us." She studied me, trying to maintain her composure, but she was clearly worried. "What are you going to do?"

I crossed my arms. "It's hard to imagine any judge sending you to jail."

She scowled. "I'm *in* jail. Gavin Barkley put me here, for life." She lifted her head a bit. "He deserved the same sentence."

"He didn't get the same sentence. He got the death penalty."

Belinda tossed that aside. "Now God has the opportunity to judge him."

I finished my tea and pushed my seat back. "I don't know what I'm going to do yet. But know this - if I do keep quiet, it won't be for you. It'll be for Brian. And for Marie, who would never forgive you for her daughter's death."

Belinda's composure finally cracked. She went pale and closed her eyes, pain on her face. She whispered, "I'll never forgive myself."

I stood. "Goodbye, Belinda."

Her voice was shaky, but she managed a grim smile. "It's been good to make your acquaintance again, Jamie. Enjoy your inheritance. You can see yourself out?"

"Yes, ma'am."

I left her sitting there in her prison.

I got into the Jeep and texted Dad. *Leaving Belinda's, on my way.* When I got to his house, he was on the front porch, waiting.

He handed me a cold Coke, and I dropped into the chair beside him. He said, "How'd it go?"

I twisted the cap off my Coke and took a drink. "The Klingons were right."

My dad blew out a breath. "What did she do?"

"Nothing provable. She paid cash."

Dad's jaw muscle twitched. "Did Brian know?"

"She says not. I believe her. She also says her son wasn't involved. I don't believe that."

"How long had she planned?"

"Thirty years."

Dad whistled softly. "Did Marie know?"

"She says not."

Dad pondered for a minute. "Sending Belinda to prison wouldn't accomplish anything."

"As she pointed out rather eloquently, she's already in prison."

Dad made shrimp and grits for lunch, and we ate at the kitchen table, talking about other things. When we finished and were washing dishes together, Dad said, "What are you going to do?"

I shook my head. "I can't imagine living with this on my conscience. You and Sarge didn't raise me that way."

"Sometimes it's not a question of right and wrong. It's a question of wrong and wronger."

I gave him a close look. "Are you saying I shouldn't tell?"

Dad handed me the last dish to dry and pulled the stopper out of the drain. "You have to decide for yourself. What I'm saying is - sometimes justice can't be served."

"I know."

"Are you going to tell Pete?"

"I already did. He suggested that I might not be remembering right."

"You don't think that's a possibility."

"No." I put the last dish away and hung the towel over the oven door handle. "But I know that's what any good defense attorney would say."

My dad put his hand on my shoulder. "There will be a trial."

I sighed. "I know."

When I got home, Pete was in the kitchen. "What did you have for lunch?"

"Shrimp and grits."

"How does grilled fish and a salad sound for dinner?"

"Sounds great."

Pete began to put the salad together. "How's Belinda?"

"She has a new caretaker."

"What did she say?"

"She'd been saving the cash for thirty years."

He stopped, salad tongs in midair, and stared at me. "She *admitted* it?"

"Yep."

"Who was her leg man?"

"She wouldn't say."

Pete turned back to the salad. "Had to be her son."

"That would be my guess." I drew in a deep breath and blew it out. All of a sudden I was incredibly tired. "If I tell, Brian Marcus, his daughter and Marie Crabtree get hurt very badly. If I don't, Gavin Barkley and Alex Crabtree will haunt me for the rest of my life."

Pete handed me the salad bowl and our plates and picked up the platter of uncooked fish. "Even if you tell, there's not a judge in California who would sentence Belinda to jail."

"I know."

We went onto the deck, and Pete put the fish on the grill. "Which way are you leaning?"

"I can't live with this on my conscience."

He nodded. "I didn't think you could."

Tuesday, May 5

For as long as I could remember, I'd dreamed about my mom. She'd show up in one of my everyday places, and I'd tell her things - about school, work, boyfriends, whatever. Sometimes she gave me advice, sometimes she just listened. When I was a teenager, the dreams occurred often. As I'd gotten older, the frequency had dwindled.

This time, I was at the beach, just sitting, looking at the water, when my mom walked up and sat down beside me.

"Hey, buddy." She tugged at a piece of my hair. "You're older than me now."

"I know. That's weird."

She hugged her knees to her chest and looked out at the water. "I like Brian Marcus. He's a good person."

"That's what Dad said."

"It will hurt him to learn what Belinda did, but he deserves to know."

I twisted to face her. "So you think I should tell?"

She continued looking at the water. "Do *you* think you should tell?"

The answer came before I could think about it. "Yes."

She turned then to look at me. "Do you remember what Kevin told you about becoming a detective?"

I smiled. "Yeah. I kidded him because it was such a cliché - but he said he wanted to speak for the dead."

She nodded. "Let him speak for Alex Crabtree."

I swallowed hard. "I will."

She stood, reached down and ruffled my hair, then turned away from me.

I said, "Mom?"

She looked back at me, winked, and walked away.

I began to stand to go after her, and the alarm went off.

Pete reached out to slap off the alarm with a grunt. I lay there, thinking.

Then I reached for my phone.

Acknowledgements

Thank you to Todd Richardson, J.D., for the information about wills, probate, and the per stirpes clause. If I got something wrong it's my fault, not his.

Thank you to Stephanie at October Design Co.

Thanks to my writing group: Becca, Bryan, Chris, Dustin, Maggie, Michelle, Michael, and Michael. Thanks in particular to Dustin, who re-read the whole book and made suggestions for the final draft.

A million thank yous to Chris, my editor. Couldn't do it without you, my friend.

Now, turn the page for a sneak preview from *Played to Death*, Jamie Brodie Mystery #11.

Scott

The string quartet finished tuning and Scott Deering took the opportunity to glance around the room, the neck of his cello resting on his shoulder. The enormous room was full of people wearing designer suits and little black dresses. The presentations had been made and the speeches given, and the invitees of the AIDS Project Los Angeles benefit were ready to mingle to background music provided by the Venusta String Quartet. Doug Fuller, the first violinist, lifted his bow; Scott and the other two musicians positioned themselves, and they began to play.

About forty-five minutes into the set, Scott got the feeling of being watched. He could see someone out of the corner of his eye, leaning against the wall, listening. When the quartet finished their selection, Scott glanced over as he arranged his music on the stand.

The guy looked like he didn't belong. He was wearing navy Dockers, a dress shirt and tie, and an off-the-rack sportcoat. Scott estimated that the guy was around thirty. He was cute. *Extremely* cute. About 6'2", sandy blond hair that looked like it had slightly outgrown its cut, a sprinkling of freckles across his nose and cheeks. He looked fit. Scott wasn't close enough to determine the guy's eye color.

Scott didn't think Cute Guy had noticed him checking him out. They hadn't made eye contact. Cute Guy didn't give off a gay vibe at all - but this was an AIDS benefit, and he seemed to be alone. Maybe Scott could get lucky.

Fifteen minutes later, the quartet finished their piece and it was time for their first break. Scott secured his cello in its case and approached Cute Guy, looking him over. His eyes were long-lashed, hazel-green with gold flecks. *Beautiful.* Scott asked, "Are you a Mozart fan?"

"I don't know enough about music to recognize most composers. But that was wonderful."

"Thank you." Scott stuck out his hand. "I'm Scott Deering."

Cute Guy had a firm handshake. "Jamie Brodie."

Scott gave him a knowing look. "I hope you're not offended by this, but you don't look like you belong here."

Cute Guy - Jamie - grinned. He had a *very* attractive grin. "No offense taken. I don't. I'm here because someone else got sick and wouldn't let the ticket go to waste."

"Ah." Scott lowered his voice, conspiratorially. "Is there anything decent to eat?"

Jamie wrinkled his nose. "No. There's some seaweed thing."

"Seaweed?"

"That's what it tasted like."

Scott laughed. "I've got fifteen minutes. Let's see if we can find something."

They circled the room, finding the entrance to the kitchen, where the caterers took one look at them and went back to their crazed preparations. Scott found a plate of cheese and a box of crackers and carried them out the back door, Jamie following. The door opened onto a pool deck, the water still, lit from below. No one else was around.

Scott shook crackers out onto the cheese plate, and they dug in. Jamie said, "Mm. Thanks for this. I'd have gone home starving."

"You're welcome." Scott held up a cracker. "Best thing about playing a string instrument. You can eat without messing up your embouchure."

"Are you in the Philharmonic?"

"Yeah." Scott raised an eyebrow. "How'd you know?"

Jamie shrugged. "You're too good to be anyone else."

Scott grinned. "Thank you. You're not a musician?"

"No. I used to date one."

Scott wanted to ask, *Male or female?* "Someone local?"

"No. At Berkeley." Jamie didn't seem to want to pursue that topic. "You're not a California native. I can tell from your accent."

"Philadelphia, originally. You?"

"San Diego."

They chatted for a few more minutes, stuffing their faces, then Scott checked his watch. "I've got to get back. But, listen - can I have your number?" Might as well take the plunge. "I'd like to see you again."

Jamie hesitated for a second, then said, "Sure." He recited the number.

Scott entered the number into his phone. "Thanks." They went inside, back through the kitchen; right before they exited, Scott pointed his phone at Jamie. "I *will* call you."

Jamie smiled, but his eyes showed skepticism. "I'd like that."

Scott walked back to his seat and lifted his cello out of its case. He knew that Jamie didn't expect to hear from him again.

Jamie was in for a surprise.

Jamie

It was a beautiful day for an outdoor wedding – sunny, clear and warm, with a light breeze. Pete's invitation had read, "Dr. Ferguson and guest;" I was the guest. I didn't know the couple at all.

Pete eyed me with admiration as I emerged from the bathroom and buttoned my cuffs. "Those pants make your ass look great."

I laughed. "Down, boy. Or we'll be late to the wedding."

Pete grinned. "Yeah, yeah. But just wait until we get home."

One half of the happy couple was a friendly acquaintance of Pete's. Kent Fisher and Pete had been in the same cohort through their Ph.D. program in psychology at UCLA. After graduation, they'd gone in different directions. Pete had chosen to teach and was now a tenured Associate Professor at Santa Monica College. Kent had gone into private practice, treating the anorexic offspring of Hollywood elite. His partner, Graham Kirtley, was a wildly successful divorce attorney. Hence the Holmby Hills address on the invitation.

Pete had been surprised to be invited but figured that Kent must have asked everyone he knew, no matter how peripherally. We'd debated whether or not to attend but decided that it would likely be entertaining. And the invitation had said, "No gifts." And Pete had promised that the food would be excellent - not trendy appetizers but a real multi-course sit-down dinner.

I wrinkled my nose, thinking of the last fancy catered party I'd been to several years ago - an AIDS Project Los Angeles benefit that Mel had dragged me to when Ali had gotten sick at the last minute. The food had consisted mostly of small rice cakes with tiny shrimp on a bed of seaweed. Nasty. Then I laughed to myself, remembering - I'd met Scott at that party. We'd raided the kitchen for cheese and crackers.

Ancient history.

I stood beside Pete, in front of the full-length mirror on the bathroom door. We looked good together, if I did say so myself. If you looked in the dictionary under "tall, dark and handsome," there was Pete's picture. I'd only ever been described as "cute" by anyone but Pete, but in this suit I might qualify for an upgrade.

Pete grinned at me as he tied his tie. "I'm serious. You look hot in that suit."

"It's all in the tailoring."

"Not all of it." Pete finished his own tie and took over mine, which was refusing to cooperate. He deftly wrestled it into a knot and pushed my hair back off my forehead. "Your hair's getting long."

"Yeah. I'll get it cut before the wedding."

"Hmm." Pete dropped a kiss on the end of my nose. "Ready?"

"Yep. Got the invitation?"

"It's with my keys." We went downstairs; Pete picked up his keys and handed me the invitation. "Let's go."

Meg Perry is an academic librarian in Central Florida whose subject specialty is health sciences. Like Jamie Brodie's mom and his librarian friend Sheila Meadows, Meg is a native of West Virginia. She is descended on one grandparent's side from the Reivers, the Scottish border raiders who were finally banished to Northern Ireland in the 1600s, and who became part of the great wave of Scots-Irish migration to the U.S. in the 1700s. Meg has traveled extensively in the UK and intends to keep doing so as long as possible. She's been writing since childhood, but the Jamie Brodie Mysteries are her first published works.

To connect with Meg:

On Twitter: http://twitter.com/MegPerry2
On Facebook: http://facebook.com/jamiebrodiemysteries
Meg's blog: http://megperrybooks.wordpress.com
At Smashwords: http://smashwords.com/profile/view/MegPerry2
At Amazon: http://goo.gl/D9VjhT

CPSIA information can be obtained
at www.ICGtesting.com
Printed in the USA
BVOW06s1920131117
500313BV00009B/435/P